LESS THAN FRANK

**Center Point
Large Print**

**This Large Print Book carries the
Seal of Approval of N.A.V.H.**

LESS THAN FRANK

Lynn Bulock

CENTER POINT PUBLISHING
THORNDIKE, MAINE

This Center Point Large Print edition
is published in the year 2006 by arrangement with
Harlequin Enterprises Ltd.

The text of this Large Print edition is unabridged. In other
aspects, this book may vary from the original edition. Printed in
Thailand. Set in 16-point Times New Roman type.

ISBN: 1-58547-819-9
ISBN 13: 978-1-58547-819-4

Library of Congress Cataloging-in-Publication Data

Bulock, Lynn.
    Less than Frank / Lynn Bulock.--Center Point large print ed.
        p. cm.
    ISBN-13: 978-1-58547-819-4 (lib. bdg. : alk. paper)
     1. Large type books. I. Title.

    PS3552.U463L47 2006
    813'.54--dc22

2006021498

To Joe, always.

And

To his mother, Louise.
Without her, there wouldn't be a Gracie Lee.

I am sending you out like sheep among wolves.
Therefore be as shrewd as snakes
and as innocent as doves.
—*Matthew* 10:16

Acknowledgments

As usual, I owe a great deal to so many for their help on this book. Thanks to Craig and Kristine Beeker for their help in reminding me to give God the glory in everything. To Lou Fiore and Dennis of Dreamtree Construction for showing me how skillful, honest contractors work so that I could make Frank their polar opposite. And through this deadline and several others, Leonardo, Letty and the rest of the crew at Three Amigos have kept me supplied with the best fish tacos in Ventura County. Thanks also to the three people, besides my wonderful family, who listen to me whine the most: Annie Jones, Linda F. and my fantastic agent, Nancy Yost.

Chapter One

I love my son dearly but I do believe he's the worst bathroom hog in three counties. I'd forgotten how long Ben spent on the simpler tasks in life, such as taking a shower, until we had to share the same bathroom on a regular basis for the first time in over a year.

I'm already getting ahead of myself. My name is Gracie Lee Harris, and I am a transplanted Midwesterner slowly getting used to a new life in Southern California. After nearly eighteen months here, I feel like I belong now—for the most part. It hasn't been an easy time of it, but anyplace where you can wear shorts and a T-shirt the week after Thanksgiving has its good points.

Of course, my friends who are natives would say that the mere fact that I was wearing a T-shirt and shorts this late into the fall was proof that I hadn't adapted yet. My Missouri blood just hasn't thinned enough to be cold yet at sixty degrees. To me, "cold" means you have to scrape stuff off your windshield and those little hairs inside your nose freeze when you go outside to get the newspaper. Here, "cold" means anything in the fifties or below, and that's when folks start wearing their heavy sweaters.

The change in weather and how people react to it has taken almost as much effort to get used to as the more severe changes in my life. I moved out here as a woman married less than two years to a handsome self-employed businessman. Then Dennis Peete promptly drove his car off the road, leaving him comatose in long-term care for close to six months while I bunked in with my mother-in-law. And that was the fun part.

From there things only got worse, other than the fact that I found a wonderful group of women to support me during a really rough time when Dennis died. The Christian Friends group at Conejo Community Chapel kept me sane during what I can easily say was the worst period of my life so far. But even they, with their bountiful wisdom, didn't have many hints on how to get a teenaged male out of the bathroom.

In fact, in an odd twist of things, I am the only one in my particular group to have much experience with teenaged males at all. Linnette Parks, our group leader and my new best friend, has two daughters just past the teen stage and launching into adulthood. Dot Morgan, who is my landlady now that I am living in her garage apartment, has a daughter as well. Candace is in her thirties, but has Down syndrome and functions on a teen level most of the time. She lives in a group home in Camarillo, and I've met her several times when she's come home to go to church with her mom and dad at Conejo Community Chapel with the rest of us.

Lexy Adams doesn't have kids yet, although not for lack of trying. She may look like an early-thirties go-getter attorney, but she'd love to have baby drool stains on that blazer lapel, believe me.

The Christian Friends member I knew the least about, Paula Choi, lost her only daughter in a car crash a few years before I'd joined the group. And the newest member of the group besides me, Heather Taylor, has a beautiful nine-month-old daughter, Corinna Grace, who also happened to be my late husband Dennis's child.

It's a long story, and one we're done hashing over, for the most part. Heather and I are still trying to get our hands on the money that vanished once we gave it to Dennis, but that's going to go on for a while. Thanks to the way he left things, his estate and his late mother's have been tangled up together in a legal dispute that may take years to get through the courts.

Of course that tangled legal web was somewhat to blame for me sharing one lone bathroom with my college freshman when he came home weekends and such from Pacific Oaks Christian College. He'd spent the long Thanksgiving weekend with me in the apartment, and even put off going back to his dorm today until he absolutely had to. Apparently my company was preferable to five other male suite-mates when it came to preparing for class on a Monday morning.

Of course that didn't help me out when he went into the bathroom, locked all the doors and took an hour-long shower. Dot and Buck have been planning to renovate the apartment ever since I moved in back in February. The original plans were for the galley kitchen and the bath to both be done when I came home from Ben's high-school graduation in June with Ben in tow.

Thanks to a variety of problems, from the endless number of permits required by the city of Rancho

Conejo to the unavailability of some of the appliances they'd picked out and that unfortunate problem at the tile factory, nothing was even started at that point. There were great plans in the works, but no actual remodeling until some time in July. Naturally the first thing to show up then was the portable—how do I put it nicely?—facility that parked on the driveway, required by any construction project of this size. Since then we'd slogged through the kitchen remodel and started, just barely, on the bathroom. At this point Dot and Buck were getting fairly peeved, and personally I was ready to strangle the general contractor, Cousin Frank.

Frank Collins really was a cousin, related to Dot on her mother's side of the family in a distant way. He was one of those relatives she wasn't particularly fond of claiming, and once he'd been working on the apartment where I now lived for a couple of weeks, I could see why.

Somewhere in his late 30s or early 40s with thinning brown hair and a gut that overrode his fashionably low-hanging jeans, Frank was crude, loud and aggravating. He wasn't nice to anybody that worked for him, and half the time didn't even appear to remember their names. I had a sneaking suspicion that the Thermos he carried to drink out of on breaks was loaded with something a lot stronger than plain black coffee, but I hadn't shared my concerns with Dot. She had enough to deal with right now on the remodeling issues with Frank. Why add one more to the pile?

Most mornings he drove a beat-up full-sized pickup truck to the job site before I was really ready to get out of bed, and expected to start work on the bathroom immediately. It was hard enough to deal with when I was the only one in the apartment. At times like this, when Ben was sharing it with me, it was way past annoying. If the early starts had meant that Frank was actually getting something done every day I could be more understanding. Instead, the work is still moving at a snail's pace.

The whole idea of this bathroom remodel was to make this a functioning apartment where two people could share all the facilities without getting in each other's way too much. I think Buck and Dot are still considering that Candace may be back here some day, and while she enjoys as much independence as possible, she's not capable of living on her own.

Even with two independent adults, the new bathroom design will be great once it's done. Dot had the idea to reshape the existing space into three smaller compartments, with a commode and sink in each of the side units, and a nice shower, tub and lots of storage in the middle unit. She says fancy housing developments call that a "Jack and Jill" bathroom and I'll take her word for it. I've never been able to consider fancy housing developments on my take-home pay, especially in southern California.

The partition walls are up now on all three parts of the bathroom, and if there was functioning plumbing in my side of the "Jack and Jill" part, life would be a lot easier when Ben showed up like this. Of course with my luck he'd still lock all the doors on all the connecting parts of the bathroom, making it impossible for me to use whatever he's not using anyway. It's a moot point right now, because only half the plumbing is finished to date. One can use "Jack's" side of the bathroom, and the shower works. "Jill" and the tub are coming soon, according to Frank. But then everything has been slated to happen "soon" since Labor Day, so I'm not real optimistic.

I'd gotten up early on this Monday morning hoping to get going with my routine before Ben had to bolt out the door to head for school. He had earlier classes than I did this semester, which was truly ironic since he is not a morning person at 18, while I definitely am at 39. But then, I'm "only" doing nine hours of graduate work and working two part-time jobs, while he's taking a full load for a freshman.

Setting that early alarm often gets me up before Frank shows up, and before Ben claims the bathroom on those mornings he's here. But today I managed to hit the snooze button once and it was my undoing. I got about thirty seconds in the bathroom before Ben knocked on the door telling me he was going to be late for class if he didn't get in there right away.

At that point I brushed my teeth quickly, hollered through the closed door to his room that the bathroom was now his, unlocked his door and scuttled through the shower compartment to my room. I didn't even see him through all of that; just heard him thumping around in his room and cranking up the music.

I pulled on clothes, then went and made breakfast for the two of us. That took about half an hour, but of course his shower took longer. The cinnamon rolls out of a can that I'd put together were cold by now, I'd read the newspaper, and still the kid was showering. I'd looked out the front window a couple times expecting to see movement around Frank's truck, but there wasn't any. It was parked at the end of Dot and Buck's long driveway as usual, and I dimly remembered hearing him pull in this morning, or at least I thought I had heard him. I'd heard some engine noises and door-slamming at some point, anyway.

Beyond that I hadn't heard anything else from him, which probably meant he was expecting to do something right away that needed two men. That usually posed a problem for Frank if he made those plans to happen first thing in the morning, because the only person less reliable than Cousin Frank was his helper, Darnell.

There had been a lot of different subcontractors working with Frank over the months since he started this job, and I'd noticed one thing that they almost all had in common. Everybody had an apprentice or a helper, or something like that, depending on how organized their business was. If they were an actual union shop, there was an apprentice, maybe even somebody working up to journeyman status. The smaller organizations had a helper, and if it was a really small business, that helper was often family and might be part-time. Almost all of them were of the same variety as Darnell; tall, weedy, pushing thirty and likely to vanish on good surf days when they always claimed sickness or a death in the family.

Darnell couldn't claim the death-in-the-family routine because he was marginally related to Frank at about the same distance that Frank was related to Dot. But he found other reasons often enough to fail to show up, and this appeared to be one of those days. I figured he'd probably spent Thanksgiving either at the beach or in Vegas—again—and was recuperating this morning. Since the weather had been only marginal in the last four days, I expected it was Vegas that had claimed his attention. It's only a five- or six-hour drive from Rancho Conejo to the Strip and the devotees take advantage of that whenever they can.

When Frank was left alone like this, he usually commandeered the little house on the driveway and snatched my newspaper to keep him company. Maybe this morning he was turning over a new leaf, because I got my paper all to myself.

It was verging on an hour now and Ben was still in the shower, or shaving with the water running hard, or something. All I knew was that the music thumped good and loud in his bedroom, the water was still running and all the doors were locked. I decided to do up the few dishes I'd used fixing breakfast. That was good time management, but probably a mistake otherwise. The moment my hands were in that lukewarm dishwater, I needed to be where Ben was. And naturally he couldn't hear me knock over the music in the bedroom.

Going down the outside stairs to ground level for the second time this morning, I decided to check the portable potty. Frank must have found another newspaper someplace, because the sign above the door latch was flipped to "occupied." He was as responsive to my knock as Ben.

Normally there would be an easy answer to my problem just on the other side of the driveway. Buck and Dot didn't mind me coming over in emergencies, or even most nonemergencies. Being that close a distance to a friendly landlady was like having family living that close in all the good *and* bad ways that entailed. Dot felt like an aunt to me most of the time anyway. But this morning they weren't around, having taken off even earlier than I'd gotten up to deliver a puppy from the kennels to a new owner several hours away.

Buck was one of the best dog trainers in Ventura County, and the kennels behind their house were always at least half-full of really nice dogs. He didn't go for purebreds as a rule, catering more towards the intelligent, friendly dogs he could train for movie stunt work or—his favorite—as therapy dogs at the nearby hospitals and nursing homes. Along with my first part-time job as a barista at the Coffee Corner at Pacific Oak, my second paid job was with Morgan Kennels helping out while they were between full-time workers.

Normally I would have been feeding dogs and tidying kennels by now, but since they'd had to get up early for puppy delivery anyway, Dot told me she would take the morning shift today and give me a break. The puppy was the last of a litter to be handed out before Christmas; Buck was adamant about live animals not being Christmas gifts or birthday presents, so they were the one kennel in the area that did little business in December. We'd played with the feisty little lab mix all of Thanksgiving weekend, making sure he got social-ized with every person and animal Buck could throw at him so that he'd be a good guy for his new owner. He was probably so worn out that he would sleep on the floor of the van in his crate all the way up to his new home this morning.

Still, that didn't help my current predicament. I went back up the stairs to knock on Ben's door. It remained locked, the music still blasting and I could still hear water running. That didn't help me out any, either. I thought about trying to pop the lock and get into the bedroom at least, but it was a fairly sturdy door. Cou-pled with the fact that I had no desire whatsoever to see more of my son than I'd seen since he was about nine and stopped running around the house less than fully clothed, I passed on that idea.

That left me only with going downstairs and knocking until I got a response out of Frank. He, at least, would open the door to where he was with all his clothes on, even though he'd probably have some rude or snide remark for me. At this point I was willing to endure either. The morning air felt colder every time I went out on the second story deck outside my front door. Going down the flight of stairs, I crossed the short expanse of asphalt to where the green-and-yellow facility stood. For the most part it was an aggravation to have it out on the driveway, where it had been since July. It was a reminder that work on the apartment had been slower than molasses in January, as my Granny Lou would have said. Right now, though, I was thankful to have the silly thing there.

I'd hoped that maybe Frank would be outside on his cell phone by now, trying to figure out where Darnell was, but the pavement was still empty. First I knocked on the door and called Frank's name softly. I don't know who I was worried about disturbing; with Dot and Buck gone, nobody else could have heard me. When knocking politely didn't work, I pounded on the door and jiggled the handle, which I saw wasn't really set all the way to lock, but only about halfway. That made me hopeful that perhaps nobody was in there after all, and somebody had just closed the door that way for a prank.

There was still no answer on the other side, but pounding on the door felt like there was something resisting the movement inside. "Come on, whatever's going on in there, it's not funny. Open the door," I said. Or rather yelled by now. That much noise set the outside kennel dogs barking for the first time that morning, but didn't cause any answer inside the facility.

I shoved the door hard in frustration and the latch slid with the movement. All of a sudden the door pushed open towards me with something or someone heavy leaning outwards in a rush.

I expected a roar from Frank, or whoever was on the other side, and braced myself for an argument. Instead the door just kept pushing forward until I had to get out of the way of the falling object cascading out of the space. Once the door was open I looked down at the asphalt in horror. Frank lay on the pavement not moving, eyes wide open, with a tiny neat hole between his bushy eyebrows.

There was a scream coming from somewhere that was even louder than the dogs barking around me. It took the longest time for me to realize that the scream was coming from me. Only the sight and sound of Ben charging out the front door of the apartment yelling, "Mom? What's wrong?" got me back from the edge of hysteria.

"Go inside and call 911," I told him, trying to keep him away from the area below. Looking down at Frank again, I knew it was too late for even the emergency officers who would respond, but I didn't know what else to do except pray and wait for them to show up. It looked like Ben was going to be late to class after all.

Chapter Two

"I was afraid of this." The detective standing in front of me looked like a television cop on the best shows; tall, dark, handsome and upset. Unfortunately he also looked very familiar. I'd seen all too much of Ray Fernandez last winter when Dennis had been killed.

Ray was the Ventura County Sheriff's Department homicide detective who had briefly considered arresting me for my husband's murder. After that he even more seriously tried to pin the blame on Heather. Fortunately he came to his senses before making a terrible mistake. After several weeks that were traumatic for all of us after Dennis's death, he'd found the person who had actually killed him. And although I'd been a big part of helping him solve the murder, he hadn't seemed real appreciative at the time.

"I had nothing to do with this one, honest," I told him, putting up my palms in a classic protestation of innocence. "I just found him."

"That's enough right there to have me concerned, Ms. Harris. Even finding a body gets you involved." He opened his notebook, shrugged his shoulders under a beautifully tailored gray jacket that might have been Armani and gave me a thorough once-over. "Aren't you cold?"

"No, I'm not." I tried not to snap, but it didn't work. He seemed surprised at the strength of my response. "Sorry, but you're about the fourth person in less than an hour to ask that."

Ben had asked when he charged out to tell me he'd called 911. Then one of the paramedics asked when he'd finished with Frank, which unfortunately didn't take long. Apparently it was pretty obvious to a trained medical professional that Frank was beyond help. Probably had something to do with that hole in the middle of his forehead that I suspected was a gunshot wound.

Shortly after that the first police officer on the scene, a uniformed young man from the sheriff's department, had put in his two cents worth as well on whether or not I was cold. He hadn't volunteered an opinion on what had happened to Frank.

"You *look* cold, Ms. Harris," Ray Fernandez said. We were back on formal terms again, apparently. By the end of last spring's investigation he called me Gracie Lee and I called him Ray. "I could lend you my jacket, or you could go inside the apartment and grab a sweat-shirt or something."

"Why don't I do that, just to make all of you chilled Californians comfortable," I said, trying not to grind out my words between clenched teeth. I stomped up the stairs, grabbed a black Pacific Oaks hoodie that had been draped over a living room chair, threw it on over my shorts and T-shirt and came back. If I'd had some of those dreadful pastel sheepskin-lined boots the girls all wore, I would have put them on just for effect.

"Now, are you satisfied?"

"That's great. It gave me enough time to call and make sure the crime-scene techs are on their way, and to start my notes," Fernandez said. He looked pretty good this morning; obviously there hadn't been enough stress in his day yet to make him appear to have one of his perpetual migraines. There were still a few crinkles around those golden-brown eyes, but nothing serious yet. What was there already could have been laugh lines, even though I haven't seen him laugh much.

He looked down at the notebook in his hands. "So,

it's still Gracie Lee Harris, right?"

"It's going to stay Gracie Lee Harris until the cows come home," I told him, earning a funny look. "Don't worry, there are no cows in the kennels here, just dogs. When I'm upset I revert to things my grandmother used to say. Yes, the name is still the same. And you probably have the address from last time, too."

He nodded. "I knew when the call came in that I'd heard the address before. About halfway here I figured out why it was familiar."

He didn't look all that happy about his memories, either. But then the weeks we'd spent in way too much of each other's company in January and February weren't my favorite times, either. He looked up on the deck, and then around the property. "The information from the dispatcher says that the call was phoned in by a man. Do you happen to know anything about that?"

"Only that your dispatcher is being plenty generous in designating the caller that way. The caller is my son, Ben. He's a freshman at Pacific Oaks now. He's got classes this morning, but I told him you'd want to see him before he took off."

Fernandez smiled, a motion that lit up that lean Latino face of his, and definitely insured that I now felt way too warm in my sweatshirt. "Thanks. At least you've started out by making my job easier," the detective said. "Would there happen to be a fresh pot of coffee going? Getting over here did in any chance I had for a cup this morning."

At least he wasn't yelling yet. This was a good sign.

"Sure. I can get you a cup when I send Ben out as far as the deck. Could you interview him up there? I don't really want him to get any closer to Frank."

The smile disappeared. "Yeah, sure. I hadn't even thought about that. Sorry. I see so much every day that I don't consider that some people haven't ever seen a dead body."

"As long as you can keep him up on the deck, and facing away from the railing, I think it will be okay," I told him. "About that coffee . . . you still take it black, right?"

"Right. Thank you." He sounded a little stiff and formal again, but then it was a murder investigation. He had every right to sound that way. I went upstairs to find that Ben was making the most of his time away from class by playing a quick game on my computer in the living room. I suggested that he shut the game down, poured the detective his black coffee in one of my better-looking coffee mugs and told Ben to take the coffee outside and let Fernandez take a statement from him.

"Cool. Maybe I can even get him to write me an excuse for my Philosophy of Religion class." Ben took the mug and went out the door, while I pondered whether to follow him as a worried mother, or stay inside because he was a legal adult and I suspected the detective would rather talk to him alone.

I went for the "legal adult" argument for a while. Then the worried mother won out about five minutes into their conversation. I slipped out the front door of the apartment as quietly as possible and stood about eight feet behind the detective, watching him talk to my son.

It was odd looking at Ben and seeing him the way a stranger might; tall and thin, with his angular face made even longer by the awful scraggly little patch of chin fur I couldn't convince him to shave off. He looked like a normal college kid in his Pac-Oaks sweatshirt and long, baggy tan shorts. Except for that scrawny little goatee, he also bore a striking resemblance to his father at about the same age. Hal Harris had been a nineteen-year-old college student when I'd met him, and it floored me to see Ben morph into a modern version of his father. He even had the same grin that I'm sure enchanted the girls at Pacific Oaks just as much as it had me back in the dark ages.

Fernandez must have heard me come out onto the deck, because he half turned. "We're just about done here, Ms. Harris. Of course I'll need to ask you to stick around so that I can take a longer statement from you once I talk with the crime-scene techs for a while. But you're free to go, Ben. Thanks for your help." They shook hands and Ben bounded inside to get his stuff.

"Is it all right if I stand on the deck, or would you rather have me inside?" I didn't want to do anything that would aggravate the detective or make him think I was getting too involved in another murder.

"Either way, as long as this is as close as you come to the crime scene while the techs are down working," he said, heading down the stairs himself.

Since I had no desire to get any closer, staying on the deck was fine with me. I was thankful that Dot had already fed the dogs and dealt with them this morning. With that out of the way I didn't have to ask permission to cut across the driveway and get too close to the crime scene.

I did think of one thing I needed to ask the detective. "Is it going to be okay if Ben gets in his car and goes to school? That's his car around the side of the driveway. I think it's mostly out of your way, and he should be able to get out." Dot and Buck's driveway was wide where it opened up in front of the garage. Not only did it span the width of the three-car-plus building, but there was enough space at one side to put the footings for the deck and stairway on solid concrete, and on the other to provide space for another vehicle. Ben usually used that space when he was here for the weekend.

Fernandez looked up, shading his face with his hand from the morning sun. "I guess that will be okay. Don't let him forget to come down to the station and get his prints taken. For that matter, maybe you can come together some time in the next two days. I suspect we'll find both of your prints around the scene, seeing as you live in the apartment upstairs."

"I know you'll find mine just about everywhere. Ben's won't be quite as many places, probably, because he's not here nearly as often but they'll still be around." I didn't think they'd be too close to the actual scene of the crime at the portable potty, because Ben was usually the person using the inside facilities, making me go outside.

Still, I wasn't about to tell Fernandez any of that. I stood on the deck watching him talk to the crime-scene technicians. The conversation didn't seem to be very heated as all of them went about their work. It looked odd that for the most part they worked around the body right there in the midst of things. From my limited experience I remembered that someone from the medical examiner's office had to "sign off" on the body before they could move it.

I wondered how things progressed from here, and who would have the onerous task of telling Frank's wife about his death. Probably Fernandez got that job, and I didn't envy him at all. I thought I remembered Dot saying that Frank and family lived in Simi Valley not too far from here. If memory served, they had several small children.

Ben came out the door, slamming it behind him and shaking me out of my thoughts about Frank. He was dragging a heavy canvas bag loaded with clean laundry, and juggling his backpack and a grocery sack as well. "Got to run, Mom. Is it okay if I go down there?"

"Detective Fernandez said it was. I would suggest getting his attention before you start down the stairs."

He nodded. "Sure. I took a couple things from the kitchen. Hope you don't mind, but I'm all out of food at the dorm." Of course his idea of a "couple of things" probably meant I was now out of food, but he was a growing boy and he needed it. He put his least-loaded arm around me and hugged me. "I'll call you tonight if I don't catch you to IM, okay?"

Instant messaging was still Ben's favorite form of communication with me. He'd gotten me used to it while he was back in Missouri finishing his senior year in high school and I was out here in California getting used to life last year. And now that he was close by, we still probably spent ten or fifteen minutes a day "talking" to each other that way. What surprised me even more is that he'd taught my mother to be computer literate before he'd left the condo they had shared for almost a year while he finished up high school. I had the odd experience of having a three-way online chat with my son and my mother at least once a week, thanks to Ben's tutoring. Mom loved it because it was so much cheaper than long distance, even if she did have to type.

I hugged Ben back, thinking we'd have plenty to IM about later, and I'd have almost as much to tell my mother. "Go ahead on to school. And be careful out there," I told him. He might look like a grown man, but he was still my boy and I didn't want him disturbed by all of this. I noticed that the crime scene personnel were zipping up a black bag that apparently contained Frank's body. Somebody down there must be from the ME's office. At least Ben wouldn't have to see any more of Frank than he had to.

He stepped back and nodded, shifted around his burdens and hollered down the stairs asking permission to come down.

"Go ahead. Just stay over to the side closest to those stairs, and head to your car," Fernandez answered. "Can you get out around the trucks and such?"

"I think so, sir. Thank you." Ben got his various baggage down the stairs without making too much noise or dropping anything that mattered, and after some slamming and banging I heard his car start.

He backed out of the long driveway faster and more expertly than I could have around all the other vehicles. I almost didn't cringe at all watching him. If he'd been on somebody else's car insurance policy I probably wouldn't have cringed at all. When I looked back to the scene below, the techs had eased the bag containing Frank's body into the back of a vehicle marked with the Ventura County Sheriff's logo and seemed to be ready to head out.

Fernandez stood watching them leave, and then writing in his notebook for a while. I went back to the apartment and checked the contents of the coffeepot. Pouring the last of the coffee into my mug, I started some more fresh. For this kind of morning, I was going to need it. And it might even get the detective into a better mood, although I doubted it.

Surprisingly, Fernandez's questions were relatively brief. He verified that the victim was really Frank Collins, which is what the driver's license in his wallet had said. "That's his name as far as I know. He's some kind of cousin of Dot Morgan's, the woman who owns the big house in front and the kennels with her husband, Buck."

"And that's Mr. Collins's truck parked out front?"

"Definitely. I noticed it this morning the first time I looked out the front window, which must have been about seven forty-five," I told him. Might as well be as accurate as possible the first time around. With any luck, there might not have to be a second time around this time. I hadn't been that fond of Frank in life, and didn't particularly want to deal with his death at any length.

"Was it unusual for him to be this early to get here?"

"It was unusual that he would be here that early without my seeing him," I admitted. "Normally he would be in the truck drinking coffee out of a thermos and reading the newspaper, waiting for his helper to get here. The helper's name is Darnell, and I have no idea what his last name is. Dot might know."

"Where is she today, anyway? We need to ask her some questions as well."

"She and Buck left this morning early to deliver a puppy. I don't expect they'll be home until some time in the afternoon."

Fernandez nodded and jotted something down in his notebook. He looked back up at me then, intently. "You don't own a gun, do you, Ms. Harris?"

I nearly knocked over my coffee in surprise. "No, I certainly don't. I never have, and I don't imagine I ever will. Why do you ask?"

His expression got even more serious. "Come on, Ms. Harris. Even you probably noticed that the victim was shot. I have to ask about guns. Of course I'll find out if he owned one himself, and what type if he did.

But your apartment is the dwelling closest to the scene, so it bears asking."

"If you say so."

There wasn't much to the questioning after that. I provided the detective with Buck and Dot's phone number, and promised to come down to the station soon to be fingerprinted. I wasn't totally sure that was necessary; it had only been nine months since I'd been fingerprinted after Dennis's death. Didn't they keep things like that?

When I asked Fernandez, he gave me a funny look. "No, we don't keep fingerprint cards once we're done with them, not for private citizens who aren't suspected of anything or have no criminal record." So at least now I knew why I had to go back to get printed again.

"Thank you for the coffee. I appreciate you sharing," Fernandez said, standing at my front door.

"You're welcome." I didn't feel very charitable right at the moment, after the exchange about the gun. If I'd known then how much less charitable I'd be feeling about Ray Fernandez soon, I would never even have given him the coffee in the first place.

Chapter Three

The rest of Monday felt strange, disjointed and downright difficult. I cut class for the day, not the brightest of ideas so close to finals, but I just couldn't concentrate enough to imagine going and paying any attention to anything. Dot and Buck still weren't home by the time

I had to go in to campus for my shift at the Coffee Corner, the coffeehouse in the same building with the student bookstore.

When I got there, my best friend Linnette Parks, who is the assistant manager of the bookstore, was so busy dealing with textbook buy-back that she could only wave and nod when I called over the crowd that she needed to come see me when she got a break. It was ninety minutes into my shift and at the height of the afternoon rush for espressos and mochas to get everybody through that last class of the day before I saw her stunning red hair at the end of the line in front of me.

"You don't look so good," she said when she got up to the front of the line and I started making her the half-caf nonfat latte I knew she wanted. With some people I would have taken offense at that remark, but not with Linnette. Besides, she was more than likely right.

"I don't feel so good, either, but I feel a lot better than Frank Collins." I put the latte down in front of her and glared when she tried to put money in the tip jar. Since Linnette was the assistant manager next door, my boss, Maria, said that she was to get her drinks for free. Linnette took issue with this and was always trying to slip money to the staff any way she could.

"Is that the creepy contractor who's still working on the bathroom at the apartment?"

I nodded. "It is. He met with an accident this morning some time after he got to my place. I've already seen your favorite detective and mine."

Linnette had been with me the day that Dennis died,

and she knew exactly what I meant, without my having to use the word "dead" or "homicide" around the crowd at the coffeeshop, which was just what I wanted. She picked up on things immediately, her hazel eyes blinking back a few tears. "That's awful, Gracie Lee. I want to know more about it as soon as you get time." I promised to grab the first opportunity I could to come over and talk to her, and she headed back to the bookstore with her coffee.

Apparently Maria overheard our conversation, but of course hadn't understood it the same way Linnette had. "Your contractor had an accident on the job?"

"Well, he's not exactly *my* contractor," I told her in a low voice while I made another mocha for a young lady with a diamond chip in her nose that was bigger than my first engagement ring. "He was my landlord's contractor, and the accident or whatever happened left him . . . uh . . . deceased."

"Whoa. Did you see this happen?" Maria's kohl-lined eyes were huge. "I have to guess you didn't, because surely you wouldn't have come into work if you did."

"Well, I didn't see what happened. But I did find the body," I admitted. If Maria heard me talking to Linnette she'd know that soon enough anyway.

She balled up her fists in consternation at her hips. "Why didn't you tell me earlier? I would have sent you home, or just told you not to come to work in the first place."

I shrugged, going back to the counter to deliver the mocha, collect money and come back to where the espresso machines were. "You still would have needed help, especially for the afternoon rush. Monday's always a bear."

"This is true. But fifteen minutes from now when the rush dies down, you're clocking out."

Maria looked so determined that I didn't feel like arguing with her, even though staying busy here sounded better than going home. In the apartment, alone, I'd be too close for my own comfort to that spot where I'd found Frank this morning. Once I clocked out I'd go over and talk to Linnette, anyway. Short of talking to my mom, I couldn't think of anything that was more likely to calm me down.

"I guess you'll be going first Wednesday night," Linnette said with a sigh when I had told her everything that happened this morning. In addition to being my best friend, Linnette was also the leader of a Christian Friends group at Conejo Community Chapel. The women who get together to share stuff in that group have kept me as sane as possible in the last ten months by being my prayer partners, my sounding boards and just what their name says . . . Christian friends to walk through the hard times with each other. Linnette had introduced me to the group last winter when she'd found me in tears in one of the bookstore aisles and I've been stirring things up in the group ever since, I'm afraid.

My first night there brought the revelation for one of the other members, Heather Taylor, that her missing fiancé, who was also the father of her child, wasn't missing at all, but in a coma *and* somebody else's husband, namely mine. Oddly enough Heather and I are both still part of the group, and when she can't get a sitter, her beautiful daughter Corinna Grace gets passed around from person to person while we all talk and pray. It's great for most of the rest of us to get a "baby fix" and helpful for Heather to have that many hands to take care of the baby.

We all have problems to share at Christian Friends, which meets twice a month on Wednesdays at the Chapel. Normally whoever has the biggest problem shares first. I hadn't gone first in quite a few months, which was a nice change in my life. For a while I was first all the time. But once I'd moved to Dot and Buck's apartment and gotten Ben settled in California before he headed off to Pacific Oaks and the dorm, my life had gotten downright calm.

It looked like that was about to change for a while, but hopefully just a brief while. I couldn't see how I would get too involved in Frank's death. He and I weren't that close. It was going to be difficult for Dot because he was her relative, and even more difficult because this meant that somehow she'd have to find someone to take over a half-done remodeling job. Darnell certainly couldn't do it himself. I didn't envy her that task from what little I'd seen of the home repair business in Southern California.

One thing I'd learned in the last eighteen months is that this part of the country has its own speed. I'd had portions of my condo worked on in Missouri and the projects were always slower and more expensive than expected, but only to a degree. Here, everything seemed to take twice as long as promised and cost an incredible amount. And nobody was going to want to take on a job someone else had gotten this far into.

All this was going to make my life as a tenant a pretty miserable experience, but that would be nothing compared to what Dot and Buck were going to have to deal with. I figured she would be right after me in line Wednesday night, and I told Linnette so.

"That's probably true. Was she close to Frank?" As group leader, Linnette ran our Christian Friends sessions and guided us all through the thornier issues, consulting Pastor George if things got too difficult for her to handle.

"They didn't seem to be that close. Mostly she complained because he expected all kinds of breaks because he was family, but wasn't giving her any in return," I told Linnette truthfully. Frank had struck me as the kind of cousin you'd never want to kiss, but that might just be my opinion. I'd probably seen more of his day-to-day antics than Dot had, since I'd been living in the apartment he was remodeling and she had a fairly full life on the other end of the property and beyond.

"Well, maybe it will all work out fairly easily. Bring it up first thing after prayers Wednesday night and at least you'll have us all pulling for you." She got up and gave my shoulder a squeeze. "Now that Maria sent you home, you don't want to come over and shelve returns, do you? I'm short workers as usual."

Normally I might have taken her up on her offer, but I found that once I'd gotten all the morning's events told, I was beginning to feel worn out. "I think I'm actually going home. Maybe pick up some fish tacos on the way and call it an evening." Fish tacos were one of those things my Missouri relatives couldn't even imagine that I'd gotten almost addicted to in California. They're really fantastic, if you like fish to begin with. They're also nothing like a pallid Midwestern taco of packaged crunchy shell, ground beef, iceberg lettuce and cheese, either.

Picking up a couple grilled mahi-mahi tacos with avocado salsa and a cold diet soda sounded better and better. I would put my feet up, dispense with propriety and eat in the living room when I got home. I made my goodbyes to Linnette and an hour later I was watching the evening game shows on TV and nodding off over an open textbook. The fish tacos had been every bit as good as I expected them to be, but putting food in my stomach just made me realize how tired I was.

I noticed that Dot and Buck had gotten home sometime while I was away, and Dot had left a message on my answering machine. "This is Dot. I've already talked to Detective Fernandez, and he told me all about Frank. I'm so sorry you had to be involved in this. Call me when you get home," she had said. Dot sounded a little shaky but not terribly upset. I guess when you've seen everything she has in seventy years, it's hard to get real upset about most things. I knew I should call, but that would mean more than just talking on the phone, knowing Dot, and I didn't have the energy to go over and talk to them at this point.

We ended up talking briefly the next morning amidst a lot of commotion on the driveway. The first person to show up was somebody I should have expected sooner. Sam Blankenship had been the lowliest reporter on the food chain at the Rancho Conejo edition of the *Ventura County Star* when Dennis was killed. Sam used his coverage of what, at first, just looked like a suspicious death at Conejo Board and Care to boost himself higher in his editor's regard. Now he actually covered part of the crime beat.

His fortunes hadn't improved enough to do much for his wardrobe yet. He still wore battered khakis and a barely presentable shirt but he had some charm that made people talk to him. This morning was no different. The company that owned the portable toilet had sent out a driver and one of their big trucks to remove the facility. "First time I've ever had a call like this one," the driver told Sam as he operated the hoist equipment that lifted everything onto the back of the truck. "I'm supposed to take the whole unit, contents and all, to the sheriff's department because it's evidence. Can you believe that? And I thought my job was bad."

I hadn't thought before that there might be things inside the unit that would tell Fernandez and his crime-scene techs more about the murder. Given that evidence and where it might be found, I didn't want their job, either. Dot stood out on the driveway with the rest of us watching all this while Buck was tending to the kennels. "Does this mean that this is where you found Frank?" she asked.

"It was. He was fully clothed and everything. It wasn't like he'd been in there for the normal purposes. I think whoever it was that shot him put him in there to hide the evidence."

We didn't say much more for a few minutes. Sam asked the driver a few more questions, and jotted down notes that I knew included what he'd overheard me tell Dot. I didn't mind; he would ask me the same questions sooner or later anyway. Dot stood quite a few feet from me, watching silently, which was odd for her. Maybe Frank's death had affected her more than I had thought. "I'm so sorry that this had to happen, Dot. Do you know how his wife is taking all this?"

"I haven't talked to her. We aren't all that close. But I talked to one of Frank's aunts, the one cousin in that bunch I usually talk to, and everybody's shocked. Gathering from what she said, I think the biggest surprise is that nobody did this earlier. If I'd known before what a scoundrel Frank Collins was, I would never have insisted we hire him, even if he is family."

Whoops. That was a lot more information than I wanted, and I had no idea how to respond. Dot didn't seem to need a response anyway. In fact, she stopped herself from saying any more. "I shouldn't be talking, I expect. I'm supposed to go in to the sheriff's department and talk to that detective later today, and he said not to say anything to anybody. Buck's going with me and we're both being fingerprinted."

"Ben and I are supposed to go do the same thing. Maybe we'll meet you down there."

"Maybe so," Dot said, with less enthusiasm than usual. She went back to the house as the man finished loading his "evidence" on the back of the flatbed truck. He got in the truck and pulled out of the driveway, and Sam turned his attention to me.

"So you found the body, huh? And he was in what that guy just hauled away?" Sam had a look that said he didn't know whether to laugh or shudder.

"That about sums it up." I didn't want to say too much for fear of the grief I'd get from Fernandez.

"Look, I've talked to the sheriff's department already and gotten as much as I could. It's obviously a homicide because there were too many circumstances that ruled out suicide. I know the guy's name and that he's a general contractor. Was he working on your place?"

"He had been. And it's not my place, Sam, it's a rental. I think to get any more information you'll have to talk to the owners."

"That's the lady who just went in the house and who else?"

"That gentleman over there." I pointed to Buck, who had finished with the kennels and was running Hondo through his paces. The big shepherd had trained as a stunt dog for movie work and could look like a ferocious attack dog.

Sam didn't move from where he stood. "Maybe a

38

little later, then. Have a nice day, Ms. Harris."

Ben was hard to reach that day, and we didn't get down to the sheriff's department. Buck had told me that he'd take over the kennel work for a few days. It was strange, but when he told me, he was as standoffish as Dot had been earlier. I was really wondering what was going on. It was almost as if by finding Frank's body, I was somehow responsible in their eyes for his death. Maybe things would simmer down in a few days and we could all start treating each other normally again. Or maybe not, and I'd be looking for a new place to live. What a depressing thought. Real estate out here is unbelievable, even rental units.

I put that problem out of mind, not willing to deal with it unless I had to. On Wednesday morning I went in to classes and then came back home before my late after-noon shift at the Coffee Corner again. Surely by now Maria wouldn't have any problems with me working. Besides, I needed that three hours pay, no matter how tiny the amount.

Getting ready to go into work later, it dawned on me that I needed to talk to Dot. Most times we'd been going to Christian Friends meetings at church together, but tonight I'd be going straight from the Coffee Corner to the Chapel. Once I had everything else together, I put my stuff in the car and walked around to the front door.

Once I'd knocked and set the inside dogs to barking, but before Dot shooed them away and answered, my cell phone starting ringing. I took it out of my pocket, determined to let it just ring unless it looked terribly important. It was Ben and I still needed to talk to him, so I ended up pantomiming to Dot and answering my phone at the same time.

"Mom? I think I'm in trouble," Ben said, sounding like a worried kid.

Several things went through my mind at once. "Does this involve speeding tickets, tow trucks or your credit card?"

"Not this time. No blood, either, at least not mine," he said, knowing what worried me the most. "But when I got back from class I had a call from Detective Fernandez."

"That's because neither of us have ever gotten over there to make a final formal statement and give them our fingerprints."

"No, I think it's more than that. He said that I had to be there before 5:00 p.m. today. That it was still voluntary, but if I had a family attorney I might want to think about calling him or her. That didn't sound to me like he just wants fingerprints."

My stomach suddenly felt like I'd been riding a really fast elevator rushing down. "Me, either. Don't do anything, and I'll be there to pick you up in half an hour, okay?"

"Okay. Thanks, Mom." Ben hung up and I stood on Dot's doorstep feeling mystified.

"I can't believe the message that Fernandez left for Ben. He wants him down at the sheriff's department this afternoon."

Dot's lower lip began to tremble. "I was afraid that this would happen, but I had to tell him the truth, Gracie."

I walked into her cozy front room, and she didn't stop me. "What do you mean, Dot? What were you afraid of, and why does it involve you or Ben for that matter?"

She sighed and absently stroked the head of Dixie, the dog nearest her, an affectionate lab mix who loved everybody. "We went down there yesterday and I told the detective everything I saw Monday morning. How Frank's truck was in the driveway while we were getting ready to leave with the puppy."

"Wow, he got here earlier than usual."

"That's what we thought, too. Buck even remarked on it. I thought it was odd he was here and it was just barely light. I also thought it was strange that he was talking to somebody on the driveway and they seemed to be having a bit of an argument."

"Oh? What else did you tell the detective?" I felt a little light-headed and queasy, anticipating what I prayed Dot wasn't going to say.

"I told him about the person that Frank was talking to. It was a man, definitely, but he had his back to us. I knew it wasn't Darnell, because whoever it was talking to Frank, he was a head taller than Frank, and much thinner."

Darnell might be fairly tall and weedy, but he was definitely not that much taller than his boss. "You couldn't tell who it was, though?"

"Not really. But I had to tell the detective the truth—

that the man I saw seemed young, and tall and was wearing shorts and a dark, hooded sweatshirt."

"Just like Ben's," I said, thinking back to that same garment, the one I'd pulled off the living-room chair to put on and go outside and talk to the detective Monday. It had been tossed on the chair as if somebody had come into the house and flung it off the moment they got in the door.

"Just like Ben's," Dot echoed, her lower lip still trembling. "Gracie Lee, I really thought he'd gone back to school Sunday night when we had all gone to bed. If I had realized he was still home, I probably wouldn't have told the detective what I saw."

"No, you were right to tell the truth," I told her. If anybody was wrong, it was Detective Fernandez for thinking that the person Dot saw could possibly be Ben. Now how was I going to convince *him* of that?

Chapter Four

Going to see Fernandez with Ben was about the only thing that took precedence over work, so I called Maria. She sounded very understanding about the whole thing. In fact, by what she said I had to assume that she hadn't expected me to come in at all today. I made the drive to school in record time and got to Ben's dorm, where he was pacing around the bedroom in the suite that he shared with a young man named Ted from Minnesota, who I hadn't seen much of in the semester they'd been roommates. Today was no different; Ben was there, Ted wasn't. He either had an amazing amount of classes or quite a social life.

I hugged my son and discovered that he was shaking. "Hey, maybe the detective just wanted to scare you into coming in on his schedule," I told him. I wasn't so sure that was the case, especially after what Dot had told me, but Ben looked so nervous that I wanted to calm him down. Besides, I wanted what I said to be true.

"Come on, let's get this over with," I told him. I made sure he locked his dorm room behind him and we headed to the car.

"Did you call a lawyer?" he asked once we were on the way. "Is somebody meeting us there?"

"Not yet. I want to see what's going on first. Is there anything else about that morning that you need to tell me before we get there?" I used the same line, as non-threatening and unaccusing as possible, that I'd used all through his teenage years. I'd always found that it worked better than "Hey, what did you do?"

With that same line I'd gotten information about dings in a car, a crumpled package of cigarettes hidden way down in a trash can when he was fourteen—a one-time experience, I was told—and various other teen happenings both good and bad. This time there was a lot of silence.

"Not really, Mom. Honest. I don't know anything about how the guy died. I didn't see anything, didn't do anything."

"Is there any reason that Detective Fernandez might think otherwise?" I asked, trying to keep my voice from

43

shaking. We were close to the sheriff's department station now and I was getting nervous.

There was another long pause, but that didn't worry me too much. Ben was being thoughtful, which was okay in this situation. "Nothing I can think of. Definitely nothing that happened that day." Now that remark made me a little confused, but I decided not to push it. We parked in the half-full lot at the sheriff's department and made our way towards the glass-fronted cube that made up the front of the building.

Inside, all the sounds and smells of the place hit me and I remembered why I didn't like being here. There was stale coffee, burnt popcorn or something else from the insides of a microwave and an overlay of old smoke vying for precedence with the strong smell of industrial cleaners. Phones rang, lots of people moved around the building and at least six conversations went on in various languages that I could hear just in the lobby.

"Come on, we need to go this way," I told Ben, motioning towards the stairs to the lower level. We went down the broad staircase and I headed for the all-too-familiar detectives' division. The door to their waiting room stood open, and Jeannie still sat behind the desk. At least some things hadn't changed.

"Hi. I know you from somewhere, don't I?" she said, looking up from her computer.

I told her who we were and that we were there to see Detective Fernandez. She got on the phone and he was there in a moment.

Just once I'd like to see the man when he truly looked

happy to see me. Something other than happiness always came up instead, usually either anger or consternation. And it's a shame because he's got a nice face. He's olive-skinned and lean and quite attractive, or he would be without that little vein in his temple that twitches when he looks like he's coming down with a migraine.

"I was afraid of this," he said by way of greeting. "See, this is why I told Ben on the phone that he needed to bring an attorney if he wanted company. He's not a minor, so I can't let you in with him if I'm asking him questions."

"Hello, to you, too, Detective Fernandez. Here we are doing exactly what you asked and coming by the station to have our prints made and talk to you. Now why does that seem to upset you?"

He sighed. "Hello, Ms. Harris. Hello, Ben. Why don't you go get your prints taken, and then come back here in a few minutes and let Jeannie know you're finished? But I still can't let you in a room where I'm questioning him."

I decided to ignore that statement, and led Ben to the area, also way too familiar from things that had happened last winter, where fingerprints were rolled onto cards and processed. There wasn't too much of a backup, and twenty minutes later we were back in the waiting room with Jeannie.

"I'll be out here praying while you're in there with the detective," I told Ben. "Just tell him the truth and things should go fine."

His eyes were bigger than they'd been when he broke a neighbor's window playing ball at thirteen. "If you say so. I appreciate the prayer part, Mom." Ray Fernandez came out of his office then and motioned Ben in. My son got up, squared his narrow shoulders and followed the detective.

I had to take it as a good sign that Fernandez was talking to Ben in his office. If he had a truly serious reason to suspect Ben of a crime, they wouldn't be in the office right now, but in one of those awful little rooms they used for questioning. They were even grimmer than the ones you saw on television. For now I had to hope that things would be smoothed out quickly. And once they were, I planned to light into a certain detective for worrying me and scaring my son.

After about twenty minutes of waiting in that outer room I felt pretty jumpy. It seemed like forever before Fernandez came back out and motioned for me to come in with him. Ben stood behind him, looking pale and a bit shaken. I wanted to ask him so many questions, but knew that if I ventured any of them now it would make the detective mad. Having dealt with him before, I pretty much knew the rules the man wanted a police investigation to go by. They didn't include witnesses or suspects comparing notes on the way in and out of his office.

I gave Ben a good long look and as much of a smile as I could muster. His in return was pretty weak. Jeannie must have sensed Ben's discomfort, because she was up from her desk, already showing him where to sit to wait for me, and offering to get him a soda from the machine nearby. While following Ray into his office, I could hear Ben agreeing to a cold drink.

I struggled to just sit myself down in the uncomfortable chair facing Ray Fernandez's desk and be quiet, but for Ben's sake that's what I did. At this point I didn't want to do anything that would cause problems for either of us. I knew that my son had no part in anything having to do with Frank's death, but I had absolutely no proof. And I knew from past experience just how little credit Fernandez would give to mother's intuition.

The silence stretched on while Fernandez took a sip of his coffee, looked down at his notebook and then up at me. Those golden brown eyes made me want to squirm about the same way my tenth-grade English teacher did. She always suspected I was up to no good but could never prove it. In reality, the worst thing I ever did in her class was sneak a novel behind the book we were supposed to be reading.

"Okay, so what's up? I expected you to be on my case the moment you got in here." Fernandez had one slim dark eyebrow arched in question, making him look sinister.

"I'd like to," I admitted. "But it would only upset you, and I have no proof that you'd accept that would show you that Ben had nothing to do with any of this."

His eyebrow quirked a little bit higher. "Does this mean you have some kind of proof that I *wouldn't* accept?"

"Not exactly. I can tell you that I'm pretty sure Ben didn't leave the apartment that morning until he heard me screaming in the driveway. But I can't prove it, because I only heard him through doors before that moment in the morning, I didn't see him."

"Okay. Then let's walk through everything that you did see and hear that morning, just to verify the statement you gave me that day." Fernandez was being much calmer than I expected. That probably should have calmed me down, but it didn't. Nothing would calm me down much until he looked me straight in the eye and told me that Ben was no longer a suspect in Frank's murder.

I went through the events of Monday morning as clearly as I could remember them. "So you were in the bathroom and Ben knocked on the door from his side, telling you he needed to shower."

I nodded. "And after that he spent at least forty-five minutes in there, but I didn't see him go in because I closed my door as I left. So I can't prove in any way that he got straight out of bed, looked at the clock and went directly in to take his shower."

"But it's what you would have expected him to do?"

"It is. Ben's not prone to wandering around outside, especially not early in the morning. He's pretty good about telling me where he is, or if he's going out when we're actually under the same roof. I don't always know everything when he's at school."

"And if he's like most eighteen-year-old males, that's probably a good thing," Fernandez said with a hint of a

48

grin. "I'd worry more if he actually told you everything that went on when he wasn't at home."

He looked down at his notes again. "When I talked to you the first time Monday morning, you went back into the apartment to put on a jacket."

"At your urging, I would add." I tried not to snap.

"True. You came out in a dark hooded sweatshirt. Was it yours?"

"No. It's Ben's. He'd left it in the living room and it was the first thing I thought to grab. My lightweight jacket was in the bedroom, and the sweatshirt was handy." I had resolved that I would tell the truth with Fernandez, even if it didn't make me, or Ben, look all that good. I had never found a problem yet that lying helped. Besides, as my grandmother used to say, if you always told the truth, you never had to worry about keeping your story straight.

Fernandez seemed continually surprised by my answers. He must have expected me to defend Ben, and I had every intention of doing that when I could do so *and* tell the truth. "Before Monday, had you ever seen your son and Frank Collins together?"

"Only when they were both in the apartment over the summer when Frank was working on the remodeling job. And that wasn't very often."

"You'd never heard Ben have any arguments with Mr. Collins about anything?"

"I never saw Ben talk to Frank Collins in much of any fashion, argumentative or otherwise. And I can't imagine what they might argue about."

That finally got Fernandez writing in his notebook again, making me wonder what was behind that question. What had Ben told him that would be a surprise to me? I was going to have to have a chat with my son after this.

"Ben seems like a fairly easygoing guy. And you said Monday that you don't own a gun, correct?" Did Fernandez think he was going to sneak something by me?

"That's correct, Detective. I do not now, nor have I ever, owned any kind of gun besides a water pistol that Ben might have had at one time or another. I don't believe in keeping guns in the house."

"Fair enough." He wrote some more in his notebook while I sat trying not to fidget.

"I take it that Frank was shot, as it looked like Monday, and you're trying to figure out who owns the gun that did it."

"Now you know I can't tell you anything of that sort," Fernandez said, grumbling. That vein in his temple had begun to work overtime.

"Hey, you're asking me questions about my son and I'm telling you the truth. I figured I could at least chance that you'd do the same if I asked you a question." It wasn't likely that I'd get an answer, but I could at least try.

Fernandez gave me a long, thoughtful look. My heart did little flip-flops in reaction. "Circumstantially there are things that could look like Ben had something to do with all this."

"Like Dot seeing somebody in a dark hooded sweatshirt talking to Frank that morning," I said. "And the fact that I can't prove that Ben wasn't outside before I saw him."

Fernandez sighed. "Exactly. I hoped that Mrs. Morgan wouldn't say something to you, but apparently that was too much to hope for."

"She only told me the truth. And I still don't think the person she saw was Ben. He told me he hadn't had any contact with Frank that morning, and I believe him. We may not have the best mother-son relationship in the world, but he normally doesn't lie to me about anything."

"Even when it would cause him trouble?"

I nodded. "Even then. He even told me when he drove Dennis's new car without permission when he only had his permit in Missouri and Dennis was sure somebody on a parking lot made that horrible scratch in the finish. He spent most of the summer mowing lawns to pay for the bodywork, too."

"I can see why you have faith in him then," Fernandez said. He didn't appear to be teasing me, either.

"Good. So are we free to go?"

"For now. I can't promise that I won't be calling either of you back in. There's still a lot of lab work to be done, and several more people I haven't talked to yet that could clear some things up for me."

"Is Ben still a suspect?"

Fernandez sighed again. "Ms. Harris, I can't rule anybody out at this point, especially not anybody who's young and male. You've apparently told me the truth so far and it would be a disservice to you if I didn't do the same. But he's no more or less a suspect than about half a dozen other young men."

He looked down at his notebook. "You don't happen to have a list of the subcontractors on the job, do you?"

"Not a formal one. I could piece one together, but I'd expect that Frank himself would have kept the actual list, and that Dot Morgan would have a copy as well. But I have to tell you that Frank wasn't nearly as good with paperwork as she wanted him to be."

"I haven't talked to half the people that I need to yet, and that's becoming a familiar refrain. It would appear that Mr. Collins wasn't as great as he could have been about a lot of things." He looked at me sharply. "Not that you should be repeating that."

"I certainly wouldn't repeat it as if you'd said it. But I can't deny saying it a few times myself already. Frank seemed to use fairly decent subcontractors. Both the electrical and plumbing guys seemed to be on top of things, but Frank and Darnell weren't anything to write home about."

Fernandez stood and I felt that the interview was over. It wasn't something I was going to argue with; I was anxious to get out of here and take Ben with me. We stopped by the front room and he cautioned Ben not to leave town without telling the police, and promised to be in touch soon. Ben looked like he'd calmed down a little, but not a whole lot.

I waited until we were about halfway back to the dorm before I said what was on my mind. "Before we went into the station, you said that nothing that happened Monday would have given the police any reason to suspect you. And the detective asked me about any arguments you might have had with Frank Collins. When I put those two things together, it makes me think there might be some reason that *somebody* would think you two didn't get along so well."

"We didn't." There was more anger in that short sentence than I'd expected.

"Okay, tell me more. It can't have been too serious or Detective Fernandez would have kept you a lot longer. But it means something, Ben."

He fiddled with the radio knobs and hunched his shoulders before he answered. "It's embarrassing. Are you sure you need to know?"

"I'd certainly like to know. It would help me understand what's going on here."

He still didn't look at me. "Okay, well . . . it was about you, Mom."

"About me?" This was even more confusing.

"Yeah. The last time I came home before Thanksgiving there was no vent in the wall where it should be in the bathroom. When I went to put it back in, I found a little hole in the wall that led to the back of my closet. And there was a stepladder in there. I think he was spying on you in the bathroom."

"Eewww." Just the thought, even if it wasn't true, gave me the shivers. "Ben, did you actually say something to him about it?"

"Yeah, I did. I caught him outside his truck on the

driveway that day, and I told him what I thought about it. He laughed and said I had things all wrong. But he wouldn't look me in the eye, either. I guess I was yelling. And I guess Mr. Morgan saw us, too."

That would explain a lot. If I hadn't been driving I would have leaned over and hugged my son. I'd never been prouder of him for doing something dumb, if that made sense. At least the argument had been for a good cause and I expected he'd told Fernandez about it.

"Ben, I think you're going to be all right," I said, instead of trying to hug him and drive at the same time. And I prayed that what I was telling him was really true.

Chapter Five

By the time I dropped Ben off at the dorm he had calmed down enough to promise that he would spend the evening getting something to eat and then studying. And he assured me that some of his suite-mates would be around, even if Ted wouldn't be. Once I was sure he wasn't alone or too upset, I let him go and waved him off. Hard thing to do, but he was trying to be as adult as possible and I was trying to let him.

Time had gotten away from me, and Christian Friends had already started over at the Conejo Community Chapel. I decided that even if I only caught the last half of the meeting, I needed to go anyway.

If nothing else, I needed to get Linnette and Dot up to date on what happened with our trip to the station, and

54

what Ben had told me. The church building looked homey and welcoming when I pulled up into the parking lot. In the nine months or so that I'd been attending services here it had become a true church home to me. The long brick building with its sanctuary and classrooms reminded me somewhat of my grandmother's church in Cape Girardeau, Missouri. The folks in Missouri's boot heel would never have considered landscaping with palm trees, of course.

"Great, you made it!" Linnette cheered when I opened the door to the classroom where Christian Friends gathered around in chairs. It felt so good to be wanted I almost burst into tears. Being this emotional all the time hadn't happened in a while, not since the worst of the mess after Dennis's death last winter.

"I made it," I said, trying not to sound as shaky as I felt. "Let me get coffee and something to eat and I'll come join you." The coffeepot still held about four cups of coffee and beside it was half of a really nice looking loaf of some kind of nut bread. "It's pumpkin," Lexy Adams called out when she saw me looking at it. "My mother-in-law baked it and it's really good."

I cut myself a generous slice to go with my coffee, slathered the pumpkin bread with cream cheese and found an empty chair. Maybe this wouldn't be the most balanced dinner I'd have this week, but at least I was among friends. That counted for a lot.

"Dot tells us that you were at the sheriff's department with Ben," Linnette said. "That's all she would say, so if you want us to know more, you'll have to fill us in."

"I said a little more than that," Dot piped up. "I told them how rotten I felt about maybe causing your trip."

"You didn't cause our trip," I said between bites of the pumpkin bread. Lexy had been right; it tasted delicious. Surely all the raisins and walnuts in it made it nutritious, right? "You simply told the truth to Detective Fernandez about seeing somebody talking with Frank Collins. The fact that he assumed it was Ben is his problem." I looked at Dot, wondering how much more to ask her here. Finishing the last of my snack, I decided to plow ahead.

"Have you and Buck talked about all this?"

"Quite a bit," she said, still looking more solemn than I normally expect to see Dot.

"Did he tell you that he saw Ben arguing with Frank one day before Thanksgiving?"

Dot nodded, looking tearful. I explained everything that Ben had told me to her, and to the group in general, and after that Dot looked much more comfortable. "I knew there had to be some good explanation. Ben is just too nice a young man to be involved in anything like this."

"Meanwhile it sounds like Frank wasn't all that nice to anybody," Lexy said.

"I think you're right." Dot's lips thinned to a slender line. "I gave him the job because he was family, and because I thought that surely he couldn't mess it up. I really thought that he'd changed with age like his mother said he had, and he was a responsible human being now." She shook her head, implying that nothing

56

like that had happened. It also made me wonder how much worse he could have been as a young man. Maybe I didn't want to know.

Dot had caught the rest of the Christian Friends up on as much as she knew about Frank's death. Once we'd discussed everything about Ben and his involvement, or rather lack of involvement that Fernandez had kind of blown out of proportion, they had me tell my version of finding Frank last Monday.

It wasn't a particularly pleasant story, and by the end of it Heather was shuddering. "I'm glad I didn't bring Corinna tonight," she said. "I know she doesn't hear or understand everything yet, but I don't want to take chances. She's babbling more every day and some of it sounds like words."

"Is your mom watching her?" Sandy had warmed to being a grandmother in the ten months since Corinna's birth, which was a comfort to all of us. She'd been quite angry about her daughter being pregnant outside of marriage, especially when all the commotion had begun over the baby's father. Heather and I had both been taken in by the same con man, and sometimes I wondered who'd suffered more.

I'd actually been married to Dennis for several years, and he'd managed to weasel more money out of me. Possibly, though, he'd done more damage in Heather's life. At 32, she's now a single mom who's lost her trust in men, starting over with a new job in order to be near family, and she had tossed close to ten thousand dollars after Dennis that was never going to come back.

"Mom's watching her, of course," Heather said with a smile, leaning her head back with her hand to her forehead in a dramatic gesture. "Nobody else could *possibly* be good enough for her precious grand-daughter. Especially when I am cruel enough to leave her in the community college day care so many hours every week."

I didn't bother to argue with her, because I could see the twinkle in her eye that told me she was just par-roting her mother's comments. I'd seen the day care facility Heather was talking about, and it was one of the best ones in the county. Not only did it serve the faculty and staff of the community college, but students training in early childhood education worked a number of hours there and most of them were fabulous with their young charges. They were carefully supervised, and I felt sure that Corinna was getting the best care possible.

At the same time her grandmother was probably wor-ried and maybe even feeling a little guilty that she couldn't take care of Corinna herself. And I'm sure she harbored some lingering resentment against Dennis for going off and deserting her daughter. That part I couldn't blame her for; I felt a lot of lingering resent-ment against Dennis myself. He'd left me high and dry with no place to live and little money. The resentment had faded as time went on, because it did absolutely no good to keep it. Hanging around with the Christian Friends and listening to Pastor George on Sundays were helping with the resentment quite a bit. Getting more deeply acquainted with Scripture helped, too.

Unfortunately, the last week had just given me a new target or targets for resentment. I wasn't sure whether I was more upset about Frank Collins getting killed in the driveway when Ben was around, or angry at Ray Fernandez. Surely he couldn't really think that Ben had anything to do with this? I know that his job meant he had to suspect everybody until he knew something different, but it was difficult to be on this end of the suspicion.

I'd been there myself for a brief while during the investigation into Dennis's death, and it was an unpleasant place to be. Heather had been under even more scrutiny and I'd seen how uncomfortable she felt. To have Ben in that spot, even peripherally, was even more unpleasant. And I guess if I could be totally unbiased about the facts as Ray Fernandez saw them, instead of being Ben's mom, I had to admit that there were reasons to suspect him at first.

Ben had spent the night in my apartment not too far from where Frank was killed. Someone who matched his description was seen talking to Frank in an animated fashion sometime in the hour or two before his death. And at least one person had seen and heard Ben having an argument with Frank on a prior occasion. Adding up all those things as cold hard facts made the situation look bad for Ben. Granted, each fact had a good explanation, but lumped together the best circumstances looked a little shady.

During the last murder investigation I'd been a part

of, Ray Fernandez had been aggravating but fair for the most part. I didn't agree with all of his ideas last winter, especially when he suspected Heather of killing Dennis. Then again, though, I didn't have anything to back up my arguments that I could take to the police as proof. From the beginning I'd had the feeling that no matter what Dennis had put Heather through, she wasn't the kind of person to kill him over the grief she'd suffered. I had been right, but it had taken solid proof in another direction to get the sheriff's department to see that point of view.

Things were awfully similar now. I knew it would take proof of the actual killer to get Fernandez to suspect someone other than Ben. I prayed that we didn't have to get involved in the investigation this time. And when it came time to voice my concerns of the evening in group prayer with the Christian Friends, that's exactly what I asked for out loud. I knew that these women would be the first ones to help me if we needed to get involved, but it was the last thing I wanted to do.

Holding hands in prayer, Lexy's warm, soft fingers laced into mine on one side and Dot's slightly cooler, dry hand on the other side, I felt more at peace than I had in days. Now if Fernandez could just find the right information I'd be even happier. A pang of guilt hit me while I was praying as a thought struck me. Whoever killed Frank Collins had a mother who would be just as grief-stricken at the thought of his or her involvement as I felt about Ben. And Frank Collins had a mother himself.

Whatever action took the pain away from my heart was going to lay it even more heavily on at least two more mothers. It put the whole investigation in a different light for me, one I thought about long into the night on Wednesday when I couldn't sleep. Maybe I needed to borrow a dog from Dot and Buck. Company in the form of a dog while I fell asleep sounded like a good thing.

The thoughts about Frank's mother stayed with me through Thursday morning as I went to classes and then finally worked a shift at the Coffee Corner. Maria still seemed surprised to see me, but I needed to be out among people. Three hours in the late afternoon and early evening passed quickly with lots of students and faculty members wanting coffee drinks and hot chocolate to get them through their late-in-the-day slumps.

When my shift was almost over, Ben came up to the counter. I made him a mint hot chocolate with whipped cream and sprinkles. "I might have wanted something different, you know," he said with a wry grin as he looked down at the mug in front of him.

"Yes, you might have. Did you?"

He gave me a real smile. "No, this is fine. Just wanted to keep you guessing for a minute, Mom."

Teenagers. But then, keeping me guessing had been his job for years, and it was nice to see him trying to do it in a positive way after the last few days. I smiled back at him. "How was your day? Better than yesterday, I'm sure."

"No more calls from the sheriff's department, at least. That made it better. You have any phone calls from them?"

"No, and I'm just as happy that it stayed that way," I told him. "Now go drink that while it's still hot." *And don't get whipped cream in your goatee* I wanted to tell him, but kept quiet.

"The rush is about over," Maria said, coming up behind me. "Why don't I make you something to drink and you can sit with him?"

"All right. But don't put mint in mine." It was one of those flavors Ben loved and I wasn't nearly as fond of. Just don't want anything else vying for attention with my chocolate, I guess.

In a few moments I was settled at a table with a warm mug of cocoa and my son, who definitely looked less shaky than yesterday. "You'll be proud of me," he said, wiping away a whipped cream moustache. "I studied for an hour this afternoon, and ate a balanced lunch. I had a salad with my pizza and everything."

"That's good. It helps to stay on top of your studies this late in the semester. And it will keep you grounded in other things instead of worrying about what went on yesterday."

"Yeah, I've been thinking about that. Detective Fernandez was really just doing his job, Mom. I mean, Mr. Morgan heard me yelling at Frank one day, and then they both see somebody that looked like me, at least to them, another day talking with him again on the driveway. With that going on, he had to question me first."

That was an extremely mature observation coming from my eighteen-year-old son, and I told him so. We sat and quietly sipped our drinks for a while. "I still don't like that he had to question you first. Surely there are other guys involved in this somehow that would fit the same general description as you."

"I imagine there are. But none of them have a bedroom fifty feet from where that guy was killed. The good news is that one of them talked to Frank on Monday morning," Ben said. "Maybe whoever he is, he'll actually admit that to the police when they question him. If so, it would go a lot easier on me."

"At least we don't own a gun. That helps already." I took another sip of my cocoa while it was still at just the right temperature. Another few minutes and it would be too cold for me.

Ben looked down at the tabletop while the silence stretched for a minute. I could tell he wanted to talk more, but was weighing his words. "Yeah, well, judging from something he said, I think maybe Frank might have been shot with his own gun."

"How do you figure that?" Ben wasn't meeting my eye.

"I told the detective this already, but I didn't want to tell you about it, because I knew you'd freak out," he said. Then he sighed. "And see, you're already freaking out. Your eyebrows are all raised and you've got that look."

I didn't bother to argue with him, or even ask what look, because he was right. "Go on and tell me. It can't bother me much more now."

"Well, see, when we were arguing, Frank kind of threatened me a little."

I was glad he waited until I didn't have a mouthful of cocoa. "*A little?* How can you threaten somebody a little?"

Ben shrugged. "He just used words. He didn't push me around or anything, just got a little nasty with what he said. Frank said he kept a gun in the cab of his truck to run off troublemakers. I just backed off and told him I didn't want to make trouble, I just wanted to make sure my mom wasn't bothered. We left it at that and I walked away."

Okay, I might be able to see how from his perspective that was only a "little" threatening. Given that he was a young male of a certain age, threats probably escalated past that once in a while. For me this was verging on panic because I wasn't a young male but the mother of one. I took a deep breath and tried to think before I reacted.

"You told Fernandez all of this?"

"Yeah, I did. And he wrote it all down, too, so it must have meant something to him."

"I'm sure it did." Suddenly my warm cocoa didn't look very appealing anymore. Nothing did. I didn't know whether to be glad that Ben had told me this, or upset that he hadn't told me sooner. Either way there was little I could do about it. Still, it shook me up.

"Mom, are you going to cry about this? Because if you are it won't help things any." Ben hated to see me cry.

"Then I'll try not to. You're right, though, this upset me. Not at you so much as at Frank. It just boggles my mind that he'd do something like that. The more people tell me about him, the less surprised I am that somebody killed him. He didn't exactly make a lot of friends, did he?"

"I don't think so. He wasn't any friend of mine, anyway." Ben sighed and finished his drink. "Well, I need to go check in with the suite-mates and schedule another study session for Philosophy of Religion. I keep hearing how hard that final is going to be."

"Then go do it. Thanks for stopping by." We stood up and I hugged him. He'd gotten past that point of being embarrassed by a public hug once in a while. I probably couldn't get away with it on a daily basis, but I could definitely get more hugs than I had any time since fifth grade.

I watched Ben walk away and then I took our mugs back to the counter. Maria wouldn't even let me wash them before she shooed me away for the evening. Since I needed to start studying for finals and finish up final projects for my classes I let her have her way. Maybe after seeing Ben I could go home and get some school work done. It made a poor example for my son if I didn't get grades at least equal to his while we both attended the same school.

Driving home, I gave everything I'd learned a lot more thought. I didn't come up with any big conclusions, other than the fact that probably several people had wanted Frank Collins dead. He seemed to have gone out of his way to make enemies of people, and I didn't even know all that much about him.

Pursuing that line of thought wouldn't get me very far without more facts. I tried to shake it off and think about other things. Before I got out of the car on the driveway, I breathed a prayer to ask for God's presence and peace. I needed both. Maybe for once I could have a restful evening at home, just studying. It sounded like a good idea. I could stop by Dot and Buck's house first and "borrow" a dog to keep me company and be set for the evening. Getting back into a normal routine would be good.

Chapter Six

Friday started off more like a normal day for me than any other had in the week. Getting a dog to join me for the night helped immediately. I was limited by which ones would happily climb the open staircase up to the apartment, but that still gave me several choices. For company, I'd gone with Dixie's sister Sophie. The mostly-lab female was the mother to the puppies that had all gone to new homes in the last two weeks. She probably felt her "empty nest" as much as I felt mine. Whatever the case, she'd been good company for me in the apartment overnight.

I got up, enjoying the chill in the air that hung around for the first few hours after sunrise. It might have been cool, but it sure wasn't anything like what I was used to in the Midwest a week after Thanksgiving. In Missouri this time of year we'd have frost, maybe even snow. And no matter what the precipitation situation, morning would more than likely mean temperatures below freezing.

Here in Southern California there are freshmen going to school with Ben who have never seen snow unless their parents have taken them up to the ski resorts. They might have gone to one of the big promotions at a theme park where a machine pulls up in a parking lot and spits cold stuff that's promoted as "snow" but I didn't count that.

The coldest mornings here might make me put on jeans instead of my shorts, and even think about a jacket, but that was about it. The crazy part about weather here is that no matter what the season, you need to dress in layers because the temperature fluctuates so much in the course of a day. When the area anywhere fifty miles around Los Angeles suffers drought, which it has for the last several years, it's easy to see that the whole region is basically desert. And like any desert, when the sun goes down the temperature may drop twenty or thirty degrees. It still makes me marvel that I'm as likely to need a sweatshirt after dark on the fourth of July as I am on Christmas Eve.

This morning a light jacket felt good as I went out to do my normal work around the kennels. Buck let me pitch in now that he wasn't feeling uncomfortable around me because of what had transpired with Ben. So we fed dogs and hosed out kennels and mostly got slobbery wet noses pushed into the palms of our hands while we loved on the dogs.

"Thanks for lending me Sophie last night," I told him when we were done. "I'll bring her back up to the house once I give her a good walk."

"That's fine. She needs the company right now." When I went back inside she also tried to convince me that she needed some of my cereal while I ate breakfast. It didn't work. Afterward we took a brisk walk around the neighborhood, Sophie trotting along checking out every bush and tree. She had a gait that looked like prancing when she wasn't as interested in the plant life along the way. Of course she spent a major amount of time investigating, but we still managed a good walk.

When we got back to the house, Dot gave Sophie her breakfast and ushered me in for coffee, which I certainly didn't turn down. I was happy to be on friendly terms with the Morgans again. They felt like substitute family to me as well as landlords, and I didn't want to give up our relationship.

Now that Dot and I went to the same church, attended the same Christian Friends group and I lived in her backyard apartment, almost every area of my life would be impacted if we were on the outs with each other. Thankfully we could still be friends instead.

"You missed a visit by Detective Fernandez while you were at work and school yesterday," Dot told me once she sat down at the table with me, her own cup of coffee in hand. "But then he didn't want to talk to you anyway, so it wasn't much of a loss."

"I expected you would get at least one more set of

questions this week, because he had plenty I couldn't answer Wednesday," I told her. "He wanted to know all kinds of stuff about the subcontractors for the remodel, and I couldn't remember the names."

"That was mostly what he wanted this time. I got out my folder that I've been keeping. I think I impressed him." Dot had kept her own meticulous set of records since she'd employed Frank and it had turned out to be a good idea.

"He wasn't too happy to hear about all the billing errors that I'd found in Frank's dealing with his suppliers and subcontractors. I think it just gave him three or four times the number of suspects he wanted."

"Were there that many billing errors?" I reached over to the plate Dot set out and picked up one of her apple cinnamon muffins. They were still warm, and I figured I better get one before Buck came into the house, because once he did, he and Hondo would both want one. Buck letting the dog eat one, or at least half of his own, would upset Dot. It would upset Sophie too for that matter, because Hondo was the only dog that got to break the "no people food" rule.

"I'm generous to call them that. When I pointed them out to Frank I always called them mistakes or errors, even though I was pretty sure after the third one or so that I found that he was trying to slip things by me and by the suppliers." Dot's nostrils flared in aggravation. I could just imagine those conversations she had with Frank. He might have been a tough customer, but I didn't think he could out-argue Dot. So far I hadn't met too many people who could.

"Did he correct the errors, or whatever they were, when you pointed them out?"

Dot waggled a hand in a noncommittal gesture. "He corrected some of them. I think his subcontractors straightened out a lot of them on their own. Especially once I took to copying Frank's information and passing it on to the subs. The plumbing contractor was particularly interested in what I had to show him."

"I remember seeing the truck here a lot, but I don't remember the guy's name."

"Frank was using Leopold Plumbing this time. I might have gotten Ed Leopold into that, because I knew one of his workers wanted the hours. After all this mess, I'm sorry I ever suggested him to Frank."

I had to imagine that Frank Collins had not been easy to work with. "Still, it sounds like you tried to do the right thing."

"I really did. Matt, the worker from Leopold, is a nice young man, and he's trying to move up in the business as much as he can." Dot took a sip of her coffee and made a face. "Ugh. I need a warm-up. Want one?"

Once she refreshed both our cups she sat down again, just in time to welcome Buck and Hondo into the house. For a change she was firm about not feeding the dog muffins, and Buck seemed to agree with her. I noticed, however, that he took his plate and the newspaper into the living room where we couldn't see him around a corner.

"Where was I?" Dot asked after all of that.

70

"Matt," I prompted. "You said he needed the hours and he's trying to move up in the business. What would keep him from doing that?"

"I know him through Candace," Dot said as if that explained everything. In some ways, since I know Dot well, it did. Her daughter had Down syndrome and lived in a group home in Camarillo so if Dot knew Matt through Candace he likely had some challenges in life. "He went through some of the job training classes that she attended at one point. He's much younger than Candace, so it must have been one of the more recent sets. And he doesn't have as many problems. I think he's dating Candace's roommate Lucy."

So there were several ties between Dot and this young man. I said as much, and she nodded. She looked a little worried as she explained all this to me. She stopped talking for a moment, looking thoughtful. "You know, Detective Fernandez asked a lot of questions about Matt."

"More than he asked about other subcontractors and their helpers?"

Dot waggled a hand. "Maybe a few more. But now that I think of it, he was focusing on the young men who worked with all the contractors. I guess that makes sense after what I told him before." Her brows wrinkled together. "And Matt is one of the taller, skinnier ones among them. He's built a lot like Ben. You'd never confuse them from the front, because Matt's dark-haired and clean-shaven. . . ."

"While Ben is closer to blond and has that awful

goatee right now, which I hope he'll outgrow soon," I finished for her so she didn't have to.

Dot shrugged. "At least he didn't dye his hair blue his first semester. I don't know how many freshmen I've seen on campus over there with blue or purple or maroon hair. Why do they think that's attractive?"

"If you figure it out, let me know," I told her. "It's not attractive to me, but I'm not eighteen, either. I don't think it's supposed to be attractive to me."

I looked out the kitchen window to where I could see my apartment. "This all keeps going back to the apartment one way or another doesn't it? Did Frank have anything to do with building your apartment when it was new?" I seemed to remember him making claims in that regard, but I wasn't sure how truthful they might have been.

"In a way he did. He was somebody else's 'helper' at that point. I'm not too sure how much better he's gotten at the business, to tell the truth," Dot said with a grimace. "When we were building he mostly pounded nails and painted, the kind of work it didn't take much skill to do. He certainly hung around enough after things were done and we were moving the girls in."

"Was he married then?"

"Not yet, although he did marry rather young. I think he would have waited longer, but he made a mistake there and found a girl whose family insisted they get married immediately. If I remember right, Tracy has several older brothers." Dot still wore a look of distaste over Frank's behavior.

That made me think of another question I wanted to ask her. "Does Candace's original roommate from the apartment still live around here?"

"No, and we might have Frank to blame for that, too," Dot said tartly. "Susie got very interested in boys and young men shortly after the girls moved into that apartment together, and I know Frank egged her on. I always hoped it wasn't more than that."

I felt my stomach give a little lurch. "But you're not sure?"

"Not totally, no. I always felt thankful that Candace didn't ever go through much interest in relationships and, well, sex to be perfectly honest. Developmentally she tests out at about thirteen, where all of that starts to really catch fire for a lot of girls, but it never did for her. Susie was another story."

"Did it lead to problems?"

"Some. Her parents had a lot of talks with her, and Buck and I certainly kept a close eye on the place, since they were on our property. We were trying to give the girls as much freedom as we could and still monitor them. I suppose most of Susie's behavior was pretty natural. But either she just didn't have many inhibitions or she didn't have any impulse control. After about six months her mother decided that they'd had enough and Susie moved to a group home in a very sheltered environment out past San Bernardino. We haven't heard from them in years."

"Wow. Sounds like it was heavy stuff to deal with."

"Definitely. The more I think about Frank Collins,

and hear things about him, the more I could just kick myself for giving him another chance remodeling that apartment this time. And now you and I are both in a fix because I have no idea what we'll do about getting somebody to finish up there."

I'd thought about that, and had no great ideas to offer. "The bulk of what's unfinished is in the bathroom. Maybe Ed, the plumbing guy, would want to take over."

"It's worth a try. I might call him and see what he thinks of the idea."

"Great." I stood up and gave Dot a quick hug. "But I have to get going. Thanks for the coffee and the chat. They were just what I needed." Like a good guest I rinsed my cup and put it in the sink and cleaned up any crumbs I'd left behind. I called out a goodbye to Buck in the other room and headed for the apartment. I probably had as much studying and catching up to do as my son, with finals coming up soon.

Saturday morning, as Buck and I worked in the dog runs, a familiar car pulled up on the driveway. The nice, shiny sedan shouted "unmarked car" even without Ray Fernandez getting out of it with a steaming carry-out cup of coffee in hand. He looked sharp for a Saturday in nicely faded jeans and a tweedy sport coat. A silk T-shirt appeared to be the one concession to the weekend. His outfit made me wonder if Armani made blue jeans. I had no clue, but if they did, Fernandez would wear them. His certainly fit him well in a way that looked classy.

He strolled over to the dog runs, and greeted us with a nod of his head. His expression was mostly unreadable thanks to dark sunglasses. "Mr. Morgan, Ms. Harris." It was hard to tell if he was saying hello or taking roll call.

We both said hello to him, and Buck made a move to turn off the hose he was using to clean out a run. I finished sweeping with the wide broom, taking care not to push anything in Fernandez's direction. Those loafers of his probably cost more than the bulk of my closet contents put together.

"I'll be done here in a minute, Detective. Did you want to speak to both of us?" Buck asked as he went to the front gate of the run.

Fernandez held up his free hand. "Don't stop on my account, Mr. Morgan. I really came by mostly to ask you to come to the station at some point and look at a few pictures for me."

"That must mean you found something. Did you find the gun?" I blurted out.

Fernandez inclined his head, and I expected him to shut me down, but he surprised me instead. "We did. It was in the storage tank of the unit we towed in as evidence." Once again I didn't envy the crime-scene tech who had that job.

"So could you trace it? Were there prints on it?"

Fernandez shook his head. "I don't know why you ask these kinds of questions, Ms. Harris, when you know I can't tell you the answers."

"If you're going to continue looking at my son as a

suspect, I feel we have a right to know things like this." It might not have been the most solid argument, but it was the only one I had.

Fernandez took a drink of his coffee. "I can see your point, but it doesn't mean I'll be sharing much information with you. I do appreciate the fact that you and Ben have been honest with me so far."

My temper flared and I felt like asking him what he meant by "so far" but I kept that thought to myself. There was no need to upset a man who could arrest my son. "I am almost always honest with everyone, Detective Fernandez."

"And like I said, I appreciate that. I intend to be honest with you as far as I can be without jeopardizing an ongoing investigation." He took a drink of his coffee and let the silence spin on for a while. "The most I can tell you right now is that we found the gun, and it appears to be one that Mr. Collins owned."

"That's a good deal of information," Buck broke in. "And knowing my wife's cousin, I'd say Frank didn't own that gun legally. Or at least he kept it someplace where he shouldn't have." The gate on the run clanged shut behind him as he stepped out, emphasizing his words.

"Legal or not, I can't comment on the brilliance of keeping a loaded gun in the cab of a pickup truck," Fernandez said. "But plain stupidity or even the other kinds of behavior Frank Collins exhibited have never been grounds for murder."

"If they were, there'd be far more homicides," Buck

76

said firmly. It was the kind of statement even Fernandez didn't argue with.

Chapter Seven

Fernandez finished up with Buck, said his goodbyes quickly and started to open his car to leave. He stopped midway through the action and then came back to where Buck was coiling hose and I was scooping out dry dog food into large food bowls as the last part of the morning routine.

"I meant to tell you one more thing," he said, directing his statement to Buck. "Your wife will probably want to know that we're releasing Mr. Collins's body to a mortuary today. I imagine the family is planning services soon."

"Thank you, Detective Fernandez. I'll pass on the word," Buck said.

I wondered whether the detective would be upset with me if I went to pay my respects. He'd probably see it as horning in on the investigation, but at the same time I wanted to meet Frank's family. The hardest part would be finding somewhat pleasant, neutral things to say about him. I was still pondering that when Fernandez left and I went to go have breakfast after all the dog run chores.

Later in the day Dot and I met at the mailboxes at the same time and I shared my reservations about going to the visitation with her. "I think you should go," she said. "You would learn a lot from being there that might help Ben, and besides, I want company. I don't know if I'll be able to get Buck to go with me on this one. He hates funeral homes and he wasn't that fond of Frank, so it's going to be a hard sell."

I couldn't help but smile. "If it will be doing you a favor, I'll plan to go. Let me know when it is and I'll try to work my schedule so that I'm off to go with you."

It wouldn't be that hard to get Maria to let me off during an evening to do something. She didn't usually schedule me past seven or eight anyway, giving the later night hours to kids who lived on campus. She was a good manager with lots of "people skills." I felt very fortunate to have this job. At some point I'd need full-time work, but I was hoping to eke out what I could until I finished my degree in counseling at Pacific Oaks and could get a job there or one of the community colleges in the area in advising or counseling.

In the midst of all this I was struck by an odd thought. What did Californians wear to a funeral? The only two I'd been to had been my husband's, where I was in no condition to pay any attention to what anybody else wore, and my mother-in-law's, where I was tempted to forgo the black or navy I normally wore to such events in favor of her favorite pale aqua. In both cases I was so wrapped up in grieving and the services at hand I hadn't paid any attention to the local traditions on such things.

Given that folks in Southern California tended to show up for church in anything under the sun, I had to suspect their funeral behavior wouldn't be much different. There might not be many Hawaiian shirts

78

present, but I'd imagine that there still would be some T-shirts, shorts and flip-flop sandals. Some people might be more casual than usual since Frank worked in construction and many of the apprentices and helpers would be involved. It was hard to picture Darnell, for example, owning anything fancier than jeans and T-shirts. His most expensive item of clothing was probably a wetsuit.

There were even plenty of people who went to church at Conejo Community Chapel who were comfortable showing up every Sunday in jeans no matter what they wore during the week. This wouldn't be the typical Midwestern crowd I was used to seeing at a visitation, or what we'd call there a "wake." Hopefully those in attendance would all turn their cell phones off, but I wasn't going to count on that.

Sunday at church Pastor George announced that there would be a funeral service for Frank Collins on Wednesday at the church, adding that he was the nephew of Dorothy Morgan—which was the first time I'd ever heard her full name used—and noted the funeral home where visitation would be held Tuesday night. It was a branch of Dodd and Sons, who had handled the arrangements for Dennis and his mother. Fortunately they had several different locations in the Conejo Valley, and the one Frank would be at was in Simi Valley, not in Rancho Conejo. It would give me a lot fewer bad memories to recall this way, and I was thankful.

I'd gone to an early service, which meant I had no expectations of Ben joining me at church. When he came it was definitely later on Sunday morning or at their most contemporary service on Saturday night. There was a chapel on campus at Pacific Oaks, and he often worshipped there instead. I was just happy he was keeping a faith life. So many college kids, even in small colleges like his, use that break from home to also break with church and faith. I often wondered if I would have married Hal as young as I had if part of my rebellion in college hadn't been to reject anything and everything organized religion had to offer for a while. If I hadn't been rejecting the church just then, would it have been as "cool" to be married at nineteen and somebody's mom shortly after my twentieth birthday? It was a question I couldn't answer, but one I still pondered every so often.

Definitely it wasn't a path I'd recommend Ben followed, especially since he was at Pacific Oaks on nearly a full scholarship. I didn't think the financial-aid folks would look too kindly on somebody who decided he had enough funds to support a wife on their nickel.

I knew that for his father and me, like many others, getting married that young meant one of us dropping out of school. It certainly wasn't Hal. His wealthy family had helped out some with money, but primarily for things that only benefited him, like his tuition. They'd made it perfectly clear that in their eyes I was a gold digger who'd spirited away their precious son. It hadn't been the case, but I'd never been able to convince the Harris family of that.

Leaving the service and going to the coffee time afterward, I wondered what Frank's family situation had been. Not a real friendly one, according to what Dot had told me already. I brought it up with her again when I saw her sitting at a table in the fellowship hall with her coffee and a couple of donut holes.

"It wasn't exactly the Hatfields and McCoys, but there was no love lost between Frank and a couple of Tracy's brothers," she said, wiping at spots of powdered sugar on the table. "The two older ones had never been happy with him for a minute. They felt he'd treated their sister badly and there were always rumors floating around that he hadn't been faithful to her."

"Ouch. But brothers can certainly be protective. I know if I had an older brother looking out for me I probably would never have married Dennis."

"And that would be our loss, Gracie Lee, but probably your gain." Dot patted my hand.

"Probably Heather's gain as well, although you never can tell," I said. "If I hadn't married Dennis, he might have gone back to California even sooner. All that is just speculation, though."

Dot nodded. "For reasons we don't really understand, the way things all happened was a part of God's plan for you. Sometimes I ask Him what my particular plan is all about, because it sure is hard to figure out."

She had a wry smile, and I could only imagine how many challenges she had already faced in life that didn't have a clear explanation for anybody. They certainly wouldn't have made sense in the way the world looked at things.

As if she read my mind Dot continued on. "Buck and I married fairly late in life, and we waited a while for Candace. Then when she was born the doctors told us about her problems, and said she might never talk, or do most things on her own. They were wrong, though. Candace not only talks, but she reads, and in the group home situation she's in she is as independent as she can be."

"Still, I bet you wondered some about why everything happened the way it did."

Dot shrugged. "I still wonder once in a while, but Candace is so special that I wouldn't trade her in for a supposedly normal young woman even if I had a chance. She's content with her life and she loves the Lord and almost never causes us worry or trouble. How many other mothers of women in their thirties can say that?"

"Not all of them, for sure." I thought about Sandy and what she'd say about all the "trouble" Heather had caused her. At least that was the way Sandy saw it. I don't think she'd ever considered the amount of heartache Heather brought on herself.

"I can think of several who wouldn't say that. Tracy Collins's mother especially comes to mind. She's not much over thirty, and look at everything that has happened in her young life," Dot said. "She has three small children and now she's a widow and her husband's business probably won't support her at all. I know she doesn't have more than a high school diploma to try and build a new life with, either."

"Maybe she needs Christian Friends." I didn't think Tracy Collins would be comfortable in our group, but there was probably one someplace that could help her a great deal.

"I'll talk to Linnette about it." Dot started to get up from her place at the table. "But not right now, because I need to go to Bible class before I'm late."

I looked at my watch. "Yikes. Save me a seat." As usual these days, I was running late again.

In the end I didn't call Fernandez about going to the visitation or the funeral. I figured that he'd just blow a gasket if I did. Dot also asked me to go with her for moral support, because as predicted Buck didn't want to be anywhere near the place. So I found myself on Tuesday night dressed in my nicest navy slacks and a sweater, driving Dot to the visitation. This particular branch of Dodd and Sons looked more like a scaled-down Spanish mission than a chapel, and there were a few cars and even more pickup trucks parked in the lot outside when we pulled up.

Inside the large room that held the closed casket there were a lot of guys standing around looking uncomfortable. I recognized several of them as being subcontractors who'd worked on the apartment, including Ed Leopold, who did the plumbing. Most of the men wore a shirt and tie or even a sport coat with clean pants, usually khakis. Almost every outfit seemed to be one that nobody took out of the closet very often.

Darnell was near the front of the room, talking to a pale, tired-looking woman with blond hair who sat in a chair near the earthly remains of Frank Collins. That had to be Tracy. Near her and the casket there were several large pictures of Frank, with two floral arrangements sitting on stands. One of the pictures showed a much younger Frank and Tracy in wedding attire. Frank had a forced smile on his face, while Tracy's was a little bit more natural. I noticed that her wedding dress wasn't fitted at the waist.

The other two pictures were one of Frank alone, probably used for some kind of business ad originally, and one that was probably a shot taken for the holidays, maybe even to tuck into Christmas cards. Tracy looked about as pale and washed-out as she did sitting in the front of the room, and there were three stair-stepped kids in front of her and her husband. The oldest, a boy, seemed to favor Frank, while the two smaller little girls resembled healthy-looking versions of their mother. All three seemed to have more energy than she could possibly deal with.

Darnell had surprised me by putting on khakis and a sweater. I guess even surfers had to have at least one decent set of clothes. He was still talking to Tracy when we walked up near them. Dot and I stood at a respectful distance in case they were discussing something private.

It was a few minutes before Tracy looked up and scanned the room. When she saw Dot standing there, she tilted her head like she was thinking and then motioned her over. "I know I should recognize you from somewhere. Thank you for coming tonight." Her voice sounded hollow. I wondered if a doctor had given her something to "calm her down" through what had to be a horrendous period. Probably not, since she had three children at home to take care of, unless some of her family was helping out in that regard.

Dot grasped Tracy's hand in both of hers. "I'm Dot Morgan. Frank and Darnell were working on the apartment in back of our house when he had his . . . accident."

Tracy gave a small, choked laugh. "Some accident. I expect somebody did that on purpose."

Dot seemed taken aback by her candor. "Yes, well, you're probably right. I didn't want to say that, though. Frank may have had his troubles, but he seemed to have come a long way from when I'd known him as a younger man."

Tracy looked skeptical. "Really? How long have you known him?"

"Quite a while. His mother and aunts are my cousins."

Tracy slipped her hand out from Dot's, not in an unfriendly way, but more as if she just lacked the energy to hang on anymore. "I guess he'd grown up some. With Frank it was hard to tell. He was still pulling versions of the same stupid stuff he was trying when we got married, and it still worked just as poorly."

There was silence between the four of us for a little

while, as Dot gathered her thoughts. I decided to take her off the hook for the time being. "I'm Gracie Lee Harris, the tenant of Dot's apartment."

Tracy's eyes clouded. "I guess you must be the one who found him, from what the police said. I bet that was awful."

"It was a shock," I admitted. Tracy looked like somebody who didn't need any more lies or half truths in her life right now.

"It should have been me," Darnell blurted out, causing all of us to look at him.

"You mean instead of Frank?" I asked, thinking that this would put a whole different spin on things for Fernandez.

Darnell shook his head. "No, I should have been the one to find him. If I hadn't taken the day to go to Point Dume, maybe he wouldn't even have died. Maybe whoever shot him wouldn't have had the chance." He looked pained, as if he'd been thinking about this for a week. I felt sorry for him even though I usually considered him to be unreliable. Obviously he regretted what he'd done at least this one time. I wondered if it meant he'd actually change his ways once he was working for someone else.

"Well, it's too late to think about that now," Tracy said. "Besides, this happened early in the morning before you usually get to a job site anyway. You're not exactly an early riser unless you're catching a wave, Darnell."

He looked down at the floor. "That's pretty true.

86

Maybe I couldn't have done much anyway." He looked around, scanning the room with an uncomfortable expression. Then he saw something and his face brightened. "Hey, there's Bobby Leopold. I need to talk to him about something." In short order he was gone, leaving Dot and me standing near Tracy.

"Are you going to be all right?" Dot asked with her characteristic way of getting to the point. "Did Frank leave you something to live on?"

Tracy sighed. "Not much. He didn't have any life insurance except the policy the bank made him take out the last time we remortgaged the house. That means the mortgage gets paid off and I can live in the house for a while until I have to sell it because there's nothing else coming in. People are coming out of the woodwork claiming Frank owed them money, too. I'm beginning to think he never paid any bill he could put off."

Dot gave me a quick look that said *See? I told you so,* and went back to talking to Tracy. "Did he keep his own books for the business, or did you help out with that?"

"He wouldn't let me touch any of his business stuff. Said he was handling all of it just fine. Maybe he was, but it looks more like he just didn't want me to see what he was up to." Tracy looked like she was ready to burst into tears.

"How about your family or his? Is anyone helping you out?" Dot just kept on with the questions, as gently as possible but persistent.

"Not with money. But my brother Mike and his wife are watching the kids for me tonight. Mike's going to bring Frankie up here in a while, but we all decided that the girls are too young."

She looked so overwhelmed that I felt like hugging her and telling her it would all be okay, but that wasn't exactly the truth. I had no idea whether or not Tracy Collins would be okay any time soon. If she was, it would definitely be by the grace of God, because Frank certainly didn't leave her anything to count on.

"You're right. We have to tell her about Christian Friends," I told Dot after we'd moved away from the front of the room so that others could talk to the young widow.

"I will, just not tonight," Dot said. "I don't think she's in any condition to hear and take in what I have to say. She and Frank have never been regular churchgoers anywhere, and the idea of praying for people, or having them pray for you, would be a different one for Tracy. I don't know anybody who would benefit more from joining a Christian Friends group, but I suspect Tracy will be a hard sell."

"That's probably true," I told her. Then I started looking around the room for some of the other people I wanted to talk to. Darnell was still in conversation with a young man who looked so much like Ed Leopold that he had to be his son. Near the front of the room in a cluster sat several older women, of an age to be Frank's mother and aunts. Looking at them I wasn't paying attention to where I was going and bumped into a very solid male shoulder.

I started to apologize and the words died in my throat.

"Well, well, Gracie Lee," Fernandez said. "Why am I not surprised that you're literally the first person I bumped into here?"

Chapter Eight

"Dot asked me to come with her," I told Fernandez, already feeling on the defensive. He seemed to do that to me. No matter what the situation, when I stood facing Ray Fernandez I felt like a teenager caught skipping study hall. He was dressed sharply as usual in dark pants and a black-and-gray herringbone jacket. Tonight he wore a tie to complement his crisp white shirt.

Clearly he'd gone home and changed between work and the funeral home, because this outfit hadn't seen a full day's wear. Not even Fernandez could look this fresh after a day's work.

"You'll notice I didn't bother to ask what you were doing here, Gracie Lee," he said, with much less scowl than I'd expected. "After all, Mr. Collins was working on your apartment when he died, and you found the body. I expected this."

I opened my mouth to thank him, but before I could get any words out, he continued. "What I don't expect is for you to insert yourself into my investigation by asking a lot of questions and giving me your opinions."

Okay, that made me a little huffy but I tried to ignore it. "Any questions I've asked so far have been totally appropriate. And right now I have only one opinion I'd share with anybody. I think Tracy Collins could definitely use a Christian Friends group like Dot and I go to. She's young, widowed and has three kids to support and precious little to do it with." I teared up a little just thinking about it.

"Okay, I can appreciate that. But maybe it ought to wait until she gets through the next few days." He looked down at me and his meaning was perfectly clear even though he hadn't said anything threatening. If he saw me talking to Tracy again, there would be trouble.

Dot would have to talk to her cousins—Frank's mother and aunts—alone. That wasn't the way I'd planned things, but it was the way they were going to be tonight. "Is there anyone here that it would be all right for me to talk to?"

I really wanted to talk to the Leopolds, and I got a flash of inspiration on how I could do that without making Fernandez aggravated. "I hope I can talk to the plumbing contractor or his son without upsetting you. We really need to have somebody finish up the bathroom in the apartment and he'd be the most likely candidate since he was Frank's subcontractor on the job."

The furrow in Fernandez's brow cut a little deeper, and then his face cleared. "I expect that would be all right. But please, stick to the subject of plumbing, will you?"

"I'll try my best. If Mr. Leopold brings up any other issues, I'll stay away from them as best I can without being rude."

"That's all I can ask," he said, the hint of a smile playing around his handsome face. He really was a good-looking man when he smiled. Too bad I rarely saw him doing that. We really seemed to bring out the worst in each other.

"Have a nice evening, Gracie Lee. Stay out of trouble." With that suggestion, or order, or whatever it was, he turned and went up to the front of the room to talk to Tracy. I wondered why he hadn't just parked himself in the back of the room somewhere to see who was here tonight. I was beginning to think that all the television cop shows I'd watched must have gotten it all wrong. Fernandez didn't behave like the TV cops at all.

I scanned the room for Ed Leopold or his son. I didn't see the father, but the young man Darnell had said was Bobby still stood near the back, hands in his pockets, looking uncomfortable. He looked like he needed someone to talk to. Maybe I was just the person. I walked over to where he was standing.

"Hi. Are you Bob Leopold?" Might as well take the direct approach.

The young man looked puzzled. "Yeah, I am. How did you know that?"

"You look a lot like your dad, and when I was talking to Darnell earlier, he mentioned your name. I'm Gracie Lee Harris, Dot Morgan's tenant. Has she talked to you or your dad yet about possibly finishing up the job Mr. Collins left?"

"Not yet, but I know what my dad will say. He'd probably be happy to do it, as long as somebody pays him for what Frank already owed him for labor and supplies."

"Goodness. Hasn't that already been done?"

He shook his head. "Nope. Frank always tries . . . uh, I guess that should be tried . . . to weasel out of paying until the last possible minute. Dad swore last year he was never going to work with him again, but I think Mrs. Morgan talked him into it this time."

"Ah." It was just what Dot said before. "So how much did Frank owe you?"

"At least a couple grand. It would be more, but Dad wouldn't pick up any of the fixtures until he was sure Frank had already paid for them. The plumbing supply place could have gotten a rubber check for all I know, but at least it wasn't us getting stiffed for a change." Bob Leopold looked like he had a bad taste in his mouth.

"If you felt that way about Frank, why are you here tonight?"

He lifted one broad shoulder. "We were working on a job together. And Dad wanted to pay his respects to Mrs. Collins. She's not a part of what happened with her husband."

I felt like I'd already pressed my luck, but I decided to go a little further. "That explains why your dad is here. How about you?"

Bob shrugged and I could see his muscles ripple under his shirt. Plumbing must beat going to the gym any day. "It seemed like the right thing to do. Besides, I hang out with Darnell some. He's okay. Frank probably owed him as much money as he owed anybody else."

Now that surprised me more than most of the other things I'd learned tonight. Darnell didn't seem like the sharpest knife in the drawer, but I wondered why he'd work for somebody who wasn't paying him on time, and I said so to Bob. His face colored up, and he looked at the floor for a minute, seeming to compose himself. "I don't know. Maybe the job had other benefits," he mumbled. Still looking uncomfortable, he said goodbye.

What kind of side benefits was he talking about? I had to think they were something that Bob Leopold didn't want to mention in front of a woman like me who was probably near the age of his mother. Given Frank Collins's reputation, I could think of several things that would cover.

Once we were driving home, Dot and I talked about our various conversations. I told her about what Bob Leopold had said, both about Frank owing them money and what he'd intimated about Darnell. Dot seemed agitated by that.

"Everything I hear about Frank stirs me up more. And it tells me that I should have talked to Candace before now about Frank's death. She's going to be upset because of it. She may even want to go to the funeral."

I wasn't totally sure what Candace had to do with what I'd just told Dot. She'd hinted before that one of Candace's former roommates might have had problems with Frank. But that had been years ago. Was there still something going on that would involve Candace with

Frank besides the fact that her roommate might be dating someone on the plumbing crew? It wasn't really my business to ask.

Dot looked at the dashboard clock. "It's only eight-thirty. Do you mind if we make a detour to Camarillo and talk to Candace?"

It would only take an extra forty-five minutes or so, and Dot wanted to do it. "That's fine with me." I could always study a little later. And now I was interested to hear what Candace had to say, assuming I went with Dot into the group home. I should probably offer to stay outside while they had a private conversation.

"Great. Then do me a favor. Reach down in between our seats and get my cell phone out of my purse. On one of the speed dial numbers I've got the phone at Candace's house. Kirsten will probably answer. She's the 'house mother' in charge. Explain who you are and ask if it's okay if we stop by tonight. I don't want to go out there to find out that Candace is at the movies or something."

I found her phone and did what she asked. As predicted, a perky female voice answered, saying "Rose House, this is Kirsten. How can I help you?"

"Kirsten, my name is Gracie Lee Harris and I'm a friend of Dot Morgan's."

"I knew I should recognize that phone number. Dot's okay, I hope."

"She's fine, but she was wondering if it would be all right for her to stop by in a short time and talk to Candace."

"Sure. We're not into anybody's bedtime routine yet here, just sitting around playing board games and listening to music in the living room. Tell her to come on over."

Now I was interested to see Kirsten, too. She sounded very pleasant and full of energy. But then I imagined she'd have to be in her position or she wouldn't last long. I thanked her, said goodbye and turned off the phone. "Kirsten says that Candace is there, playing board games and listening to music. In fact, she said for you to come on over."

"Good. I'm not sure she'll be happy to see me once she sees why I'm there. I don't want to stir up the girls, but the news probably will."

Dot stayed on the freeway from Simi Valley past the exits for Rancho Conejo, switched freeways and headed on toward Camarillo on the 101. We took one of the first exits for that city and were soon in a residential area of pleasant but not palatial homes. She pulled up to a ranch-style house on a corner. There was light in almost all of the front windows.

She looked over at me. "Of course you're coming in with me. I wouldn't dream of leaving you out here alone. Besides, I might want reinforcements, depending on how the conversation with Candace goes."

"Okay." If Dot wanted me inside, I would be more than happy to go. We went up the front walk and Dot rang the bell. I could hear music playing inside, and the sounds of laughter. Then the door opened and a young woman with pale blond hair motioned us to come in.

Southern California was certainly full of Scandinavian-looking women. And they all seemed to be a size two.

"Hi, Dot. Is this your friend who made the phone call for you? Thanks for not calling yourself while you were driving. I worry about people who do that."

"You don't have to worry about me. I don't use that thing if I'm driving unless it's a true emergency. Kirsten, this is my friend Gracie Lee Harris. She just went to a visitation at Dodd and Sons with me and when we talked afterward I came to the conclusion that I needed to tell Candace about her cousin's death. They weren't very close, but she might want to go to the funeral tomorrow."

Kirsten tilted her head in thought. On her it looked charming. "Okay. She and Lucy and Tina are over at the table playing dominoes and listening to Barry Manilow."

Dot laughed softly. "Let me guess. It was Tina's turn to pick the music."

Kirsten smiled, revealing even white teeth and making her blue eyes sparkle. "You got it." She looked at me. "Tina only has one favorite artist. Barry Manilow. I think I now know all the words to 'Copacabana' by heart."

I groaned internally, knowing now that there was no way I could do Kirsten's job as cheerfully and calmly as she did it. Still smiling, the young woman pointed me toward the table where Dot had claimed the fourth seat. I recognized Candace from seeing her at church. She was a bit shorter and wider than Dot, with brown hair and glasses. Her features didn't have the most obvious cast of some people I'd known with Down syndrome. A casual look at Candace might show a stranger just a slightly heavy, plainly dressed young woman. Only close observation, and hearing her somewhat slow speech, would tell someone of her disability.

She had gotten up to hug Dot. "This is a surprise, Mom. It's Tuesday night. You never come over on Tuesday night. *What* is going on?"

Dot flashed a brief smile and Candace went back to her seat. "I have some bad news that I want to tell you in person, Candace."

Her daughter looked worried. "Did something happen to Daddy? Or my Dixie dog?"

"No, they're both fine, Candace. Do you remember my cousin Frank?"

Candace's expression went from worried to troubled. Standing behind Dot, I also noticed that one of her domino-playing companions had stopped playing and was intent on the conversation. This young woman was younger than Candace and strikingly beautiful. She was a little heavyset, and tried to conceal that with loose sweats, but her face was lovely. She had huge brown eyes with long dark lashes, and glossy black hair. And right now her lower lip was trembling a little.

"I remember Frank," Candace said, a little louder than necessary. "Did something happen to him, Mom? I hope it did. He's not a nice man."

Dot looked a little surprised by her daughter's vehemence. "Yes, something happened to him. He had an accident and he died, Candace. There will be funeral services for him at church tomorrow morning. Do you want to go?"

Candace shook her head. "No. I have to work tomorrow and I don't want to ask for a day off. And you said that we go to funerals because we're sad when somebody dies. I don't think I'm sad about Frank."

Candace was usually pretty blunt, but I'd never heard her express a hurtful thought about anybody before. She was the kind of person who bent down and took earthworms off the sidewalk so they wouldn't dry up before they got to a strip of grass. The more I heard people talk about Frank Collins, the more I wondered about all the parts of his life I hadn't been privy to. He certainly engendered a lot of hard feelings in the people he dealt with. This was, as the kids would say, one bad dude.

"I want to go to the funeral, Candace's mom. Will you take me?" Dot looked almost as surprised by the other woman's request as she had at Candace's outburst.

"Sure, Lucy. I'd be happy to take you. Can you get off work tomorrow? I don't want to get you in trouble."

"Wednesday is my day off. I don't have to go in," Lucy said. As I looked at Lucy more closely I could see one thing that might explain why she was living in a group home when at first she looked perfectly normal. The right side of her head didn't appear to be shaped the same way as the left, making a shallow curved indentation under her black hair. Perhaps she'd suffered brain damage at some point. When we were alone I would ask Dot about it.

"All right, then there's no problem with you going," Dot said and paused a moment. "Did you know about Frank before I came tonight?" Dot's question struck me as a little strange until I remembered that she had told me before that Lucy was dating a young man apprenticed to the plumber. I had probably seen Matt without really knowing it when the kitchen in the apartment was being reworked. I tried to think back to Leopold's crew, but couldn't remember what he or his helpers looked like.

Lucy looked down at the table. "I knew. Matt told me. He's going to go tomorrow, too. I want to sit with him."

"I think that can be arranged," Dot said. Suddenly she looked back at me. "Goodness, where are my manners? Gracie Lee, this is Candace's roommate Lucy, and across the table from me is their friend Tina. Lucy and Tina, this is my friend Gracie Lee. She goes to my church, and lives in the apartment where Candace used to live a few years ago."

"Hi, Gracie Lee," Lucy said. Tina looked up at me and then looked at Lucy while she scowled slightly. On her thin, slightly pinched face it wasn't an attractive expression. Tina looked a little older than the other two, with short, straw-blond hair and faded blue eyes. I noticed that the dominoes in front of them all were the kids version that had pictures instead of dots to count. It was probably easier for some of them to manage.

Tina was still scowling. "Are you going to play dominoes or not, Lucy? It's your turn."

99

Lucy waved one hand. "In a minute, Tina. If you want to play right now, ask Kirsten to play for me. I need to talk to Candace's mom."

Lucy's smooth forehead wrinkled in thought. "About what Candace said before. Do I have to be sad that Frank is dead to go to his funeral? 'Cause I'm not very sad, just a little bit."

The corners of Dot's mouth twitched as if she was trying to stifle a smile. "You can be as sad as you want to be, Lucy, whether that's a little or a lot. If you want to go to the funeral, I'll take you. Can you be ready about nine-thirty?"

Lucy nodded. "Tell Kirsten I'm going so she can remind me to get up on time. I don't get up very early on my day off. I like to sleep in."

"I'll do that. And now we should let you three go back to your domino game," Dot said. She got up from the table and went behind Candace, putting her arms around her daughter for a hug while she sat. "Goodbye, sweet girl. If you change your mind you can come with Lucy tomorrow."

Candace shook her head, concentrating on the dominoes in front of her. "I told you, Mom. I have to work tomorrow. And I don't want to go. Good night." She looked up quickly at her mother and smiled a little. "Sleep tight."

"Don't let the bedbugs bite. See you in the morning light," Dot answered back. "But only if I get here before you go to work. I'll go talk to Kirsten. I'm letting them go back to the game now, Tina."

"Good. I have to get ready for bed soon," Tina said. "It's *still* your turn, Lucy." In a moment the women at the table were again concentrating on their game. We went across the room to where Kirsten sat, looking like she was grading a stack of papers.

"Do you teach?" I asked her, motioning to the papers.

"I sub some. I'm getting my teaching credential so I can go full-time. Plus some of the clients here benefit from a brush-up once in a while, so I bring worksheets home at night for them, too."

Dot filled her in on the plans for the morning and afterward Kirsten showed us to the door.

When we got into the car, Dot didn't start up the engine right away. I turned to ask her what was happening and it surprised me to see that she was crying. "Okay, what's up?" I asked, patting her hand. It was unlike her to cry and I needed to know which part of what happened in the house had upset my friend so much.

Chapter Nine

Dot got more composed after she sat for a minute. She took the tissue that I had pulled from the box sitting between our seats. "What part of all that got me upset? There were several things, to tell the truth. Candace didn't react the way I expected her to at all. And Lucy wanting to go with me . . . I didn't expect that, either."

She used the tissue again and sighed. "Even some of the sweet things about tonight upset me. The way Candace slipped right into our little bedtime rhyme. I miss having her close to me, but I know she's so much better off where she is. I still worry, though. Doesn't every mother?"

"I know I do. Almost every parent I know worries about their kids. Edna was worrying about Dennis when he was over forty and she was in her seventies. I don't think it stops."

"Until we're dead," Dot said wryly. "Then at least we can give the worries over to Jesus the way I have so much trouble doing in this life. Struggling with that always makes me think that I could be so much better as a Christian."

"I have a feeling that everybody has problems like that. Now, should I drive home or are you up to it?"

Dot used her tissue one last time and put it down. "I'm up to it. That little bout of tears caught me by surprise, I guess. But it's over now and we can get on with other things. I better get us home if we're going to get up and ready for that funeral tomorrow."

"Do you want me to go with you and Lucy? If you like, I can do it."

"But it would mean that you'd have to cut class, and maybe miss a little work, right?" Dot started the car and checked the street before she pulled out of our parking space in front of the house.

"It would. But for you, Dot, I'd do it."

"This time you don't have to, Gracie Lee. It's very nice of you to offer, but I think Lucy and I will be just fine together."

"She's a very pretty girl. Has she lived at the group home very long?"

"Less than a year. I think she's their newest resident. There are three women you didn't see tonight, Tina's roommate and two others. They must have been off doing something together with one of the aides. Lucy has a sad story, but then I suppose everybody there does in their own way."

Dot merged onto the freeway now and I held off asking her any more questions until she got a little farther along. "Did Lucy's situation change at home to bring her there with the others, or was she already living somewhere else?"

"She lived with her sister, who's a lot older than Lucy is. The sister got a promotion at work at the hospital in Thousand Oaks, and she was afraid that Lucy wouldn't get enough attention. Plus, she may have just needed a break. She's raised Lucy since she was eight."

"Wow. That is quite a burden. How did she manage?"

"Very well for somebody who was only in her first year of college at the time. Lucy and her parents were involved in a bad auto accident. Her parents were killed outright, and Lucy suffered a head injury that left her with brain damage."

I shook my head, and then realized that Dot probably couldn't see what I was doing while she concentrated on driving in the dark. "That *is* sad. Did the sister at least have some kind of faith to pull her through?"

"They were churchgoers. Estella hasn't shared a lot with me, and I don't feel I know her well enough to push the subject too far. I think she'd be another good candidate for Christian Friends if she could find a group that met while she wasn't working. She's a critical-care nurse at the hospital and puts in some very long hours, often on twelve-hour shifts."

"I can just imagine." We were nearing home now and I found myself looking forward to a little bit of studying and a warm bed. For a change I had a relatively normal day to look forward to tomorrow and that sounded very good.

When we pulled into the driveway Dot and I talked for a little while longer, then went our separate ways. Once I settled into the apartment I wished I'd gotten Sophie again to keep me company. But by then I'd already put on ratty old sweats and slippers and made a cup of tea, so instead of going out and getting a dog I just hunkered down with my books. I knew I wouldn't sleep as well alone tonight, but I was too tired to exert myself to get company.

Wednesday almost flew by at school. I had two classes to attend and a four-hour shift at the Coffee Corner. Halfway into my shift I looked up and Linnette stood in line two customers from the front. By the time I could wait on her there wasn't much of anybody behind her and we were able chat for a moment.

"What does your evening look like?" she asked, taking her latte.

"I've got to put in some time studying for finals, but I'm fairly flexible. What do you have in mind?"

"I'd like to do a partial Christian Friends get-together. Lexy and Heather can't make it, and I couldn't even reach Paula but I know Dot went to that funeral today and I think she wants to talk about it. I thought maybe the three of us could go out someplace casual and have dinner or dessert together and hang out."

It sounded very good to me and I told her so. "Let me know when and where and I'll be there."

"I'll call Dot while I'm still on break and set things up." Linnette took her coffee and headed back toward the bookstore. I knew she'd been busy lately with the end of the semester book buy-back program. Not everybody waited until finals were over to sell their unwanted textbooks. Personally I wanted to squeeze every drop of knowledge I could out of the expensive things before I gave any of them up. Even buying books used meant a pretty hefty expense. The first two times I had to buy graduate school books I nearly lost it. And if I had been stunned, it was nothing to the way Ben reacted his first trip through the bookstore.

He'd called me afterward, nearly foaming at the mouth. "Mom! My books cost, like, three hundred dollars and I didn't get all of them that I needed," he'd said with a note of panic. Maybe he expected sympathy, but I'd told him to get used to it, that almost every semester would be like that. I could tell he didn't want to believe me. Within days some sophomores and juniors in his dorm said the same thing. Them, he believed. Of course, everything always carries more weight from a total stranger than one's mother.

Then, as if thinking about him drew him to the coffee shop, there was Ben in front of me. "Hey. Think you can make me a hot chocolate on my study break? Maybe it better be mint mocha instead. More caffeine." He grinned at me and I wanted to reach over the counter and hug him, but refrained.

"Sure. With whipped cream or without?" He looked less stressed than I'd seen him any time in the last two weeks, which made me feel relieved.

"With, of course. And chocolate sprinkles if you've got them."

"I've got something close," I told him, starting to work on his mocha. In a minute or so it was done and sitting in front of him crowned with plenty of whipped cream and shaved chocolate. For a change I let him give me his student meal card and I ran it through the machine that debited his account for the mocha. Maria almost always insisted on making his drinks for free, but I didn't think that was fair every time and Ben agreed with me.

"Sorry I can't take my break while you're here, but you can see that I'm alone." Maria had left forty-five minutes before, making a supply and bank run. Naturally, I'd been busy ever since. This was the first time that students and faculty weren't lined up to get coffee and treats.

"That's okay, Mom. I really *am* just on a study break before my last classes of the semester. I wanted to stop in and say hi, though. I'm glad you're here."

"Me, too." I considered seeing Ben almost every day

one of the perks of the job. He might think otherwise sometimes, but it was nice to see that he still needed me occasionally. "So, when is your first final?"

He wrinkled his nose. "Friday, ten o'clock. I think it's going to be the toughest one, too. Good ol' Philosophy of Religion. My favorite."

"Any others that day?"

He shook his head. "Nope. One on Monday, and two on Tuesday, so at least that's pretty good. How about you?"

"Friday daytime, Monday night and Tuesday night," I told him. "Spread out nicely and Friday is really just turning in a final project." Of course I'd been working on that final project more hours than he'd be likely to study for most of his tests put together, but I didn't want to tell him that. No sense scaring a freshman who hadn't even had a set of college finals yet.

"Cool. Okay if I come over this weekend? I'm pretty sure the apartment will be a lot quieter than the dorm to study in."

"Be my guest. We can study together. Now go drink that before it cools off."

"Yeah, definitely. Thanks, Mom." He reached halfway over the counter and gave me a brief hug. Given his height he could reach that way much easier than I could. It felt good watching him stroll off looking happy again. I prayed silently asking God to keep him safe, and to help bring to light what really happened to Frank Collins, for the sake of his family and my own. Somewhere there was a family for whom the truth wouldn't bring peace, but for many of us knowing the truth would be the only peace we'd get out of a bad situation.

While I mused over that and made a couple of lattes for two professors who barely looked up from their discussion with each other to take them, Linnette sidled up behind them. The profs finally retreated to a table to continue their conversation and Linnette came up to the counter. "Six-thirty at Sally's Deli. Is that okay with you?"

"Sounds great. I'll meet you there," I told her. Sally's was a big place where the menu went on for pages, so everyone could get what they wanted. It also had lots of booths and tables off in little nooks, meaning we could talk without constant interruption or worries of anyone overhearing what we said.

The rest of my shift was just busy enough to make the time go by, but I wasn't ever overworked. Maria came back soon after Linnette's last visit and at six Rico, one of the student workers, came to take my place at the counter. We exchanged pleasantries for a few minutes and then he got busy and I left.

Sally's Deli wasn't all that far from campus and traffic around Rancho Conejo was surprisingly light for rush hour on a weekday. I made it to the restaurant in plenty of time. When I went in, Linnette waved from a secluded corner table, where I joined her. She handed me a menu that looked like a small-town phone book and we discussed what we might get for ten minutes until Dot joined us. I'd gotten into the salad section when Linnette looked up over her reading glasses.

"I just realized that you weren't there for the start of the meeting last week."

"That's right. Did I miss something?"

"One thing that I keep forgetting to tell you. We have a different meeting schedule in December. We'll meet the next two Sunday nights instead of Wednesdays. It frees everybody up for Christmas and travel that way."

"Works for me," I told her, just in time to see Dot heading for the table.

"Hi, ladies. It's great to see a couple of friendly faces." She sat down at the table, probably still wearing the outfit she'd worn to Frank's funeral. The tailored pants outfit was a deep green that suited her well. Still, Dot looked tired, with faint dark smudges under her eyes.

"Was the funeral that bad, or has there been more today?" Linnette asked.

"It was mostly the funeral. I took Lucy, Candace's roommate with me, which felt odd without Candace along. Oh, and I saw that young reporter again. He mostly sat in the back and seemed to take notes. I didn't see him talk to anybody."

For that I felt thankful. Sam wasn't the pushy type, but nobody should have reporters intrude on an event like a funeral. Dot went on with her story. "After the services I took Lucy back to her place while those that wanted to went to the cemetery. Eventually I met up with them at Frank's mother's house." Dot wrinkled her nose and looked longingly at my water glass.

I pushed it over to her. "Go ahead. I haven't touched that one yet and the server will bring another one as soon as we get his attention."

"Normally I'd argue, but I'm tired and thirsty so I'll take you up on your offer." I didn't want to press her for details of her day, knowing that Linnette is even better than I am at leading questions. Besides, Dot didn't usually need to have many questions directed to her. Once she rested a little and ordered dinner, she'd tell us anything we needed to know.

We got Dot her own cold drink and replaced my water when the server came back, and then Linnette and I proceeded to order while Dot looked at the menu another minute. By the time we had finished ordering she was ready as well. "Just soup and a dinner salad," she told the server. "I'm saving room for dessert. Something large and chocolate."

After he had left the table I looked at Dot. "Okay, now I know it must have been a rough day, if you're already anticipating chocolate therapy."

She grinned. "You bet. After dealing with Ruth Collins and her sisters, there probably isn't enough chocolate in this restaurant to really make me feel better, but dessert is a start."

"What did they do that was so awful?" Linnette was the one to ask this time so I didn't have to.

Dot sighed. "It wasn't what they did as much as what they *didn't* do. I know every mother thinks her child is perfect, but Ruth is downright awful to Tracy. And the only one of the grandkids she seems to pay any attention to is Frankie."

"Ouch." Linnette reached for the breadbasket that our server had put on the table. "That has to be hard on Tracy on two counts. She has to deal with upset kids and her mother-in-law at the same time."

"And she's not managing any of it well. She mostly sat at Ruth's dining-room table and cried while I was there. I sat next to her and talked some since nobody else was paying her much attention. Frank's books are as big a mess as you'd expect them to be, and she's already started getting calls from people who want money."

Linnette looked up from the warm roll she was buttering. "She could sure use some support. I know they were nominally members at our church. Do you think she'd be open to our Christian Friends group?"

Dot shook her head. "Some other group would probably be better. Perhaps one that focuses on younger women or grief issues."

"And perhaps one that I'm not in," I said. It was what Dot was thinking, I was sure. Neither Tracy nor I would be quite comfortable together if she ever found out that Ben was a suspect in her husband's murder, no matter how wrong the police were for suspecting him.

"You've got a point there. Both of you do. I think our group probably has its quota of widows right now. And Tracy would probably benefit from a group that could deal with her grief and put her on the right track to settling Frank's tangled business affairs. I'll talk to Pastor George and see if he has any suggestions."

"That would be nice." I helped myself to one of those warm rolls. I didn't really need to dip into the bread-basket, but comfort food sounded good. "What about having Lucy at the funeral? Did it feel strange just because Candace wasn't there?"

"No, there was more. We were right about one thing. The minute we got there she started looking around for Matt. When she saw him, she wanted to sit next to him. Of course I didn't mind that. I took her over to the row where he was sitting and sat there myself, a few places down from them."

Dot was quiet for a minute. I noticed that her roll was the only one untouched, except for it having been torn in pieces and pushed around her bread plate. "I suppose I should call back Detective Fernandez about what I heard and saw, but I just hate to do it."

"What do you mean?"

She looked at me and her eyes were still so tired. "After getting Ben in trouble I don't want to make another mistake. But Matt and Lucy were talking just loudly enough that I could hear them. When the service was almost over Lucy started crying as they took the casket out of the sanctuary. Matt reached over and patted her hand. 'See, Lucy,' he said. 'I promised you he wouldn't bother you again.'" She looked down at the table again. "That wasn't all, either. I saw his hand while he was patting her. His knuckles were all scraped and starting to heal as if he'd been in a fistfight."

Now I was worried, too. "You're probably right, Dot. Fernandez would want to know about that. But what if what you heard didn't mean what you thought it did? Then another kid goes through what Ben has."

"I know." Dot looked troubled. "I think when dinner is over we should go somewhere quieter and pray together. I need some help with figuring out what I should tell that detective."

"We can certainly pray with you, Dot. And personally, I wouldn't even mind doing it here." The server was probably a little startled to see the three of us praying together when he brought our food, but if he was he hid it well. I figured it probably wasn't the most unusual thing he'd seen in the busy deli. Besides, it gave Dot enough peace that she could have a good dinner and then split one of their huge pieces of German chocolate cake with the rest of us. Nobody really needed dessert, but that cake was probably the highlight of the day for all three of us.

Chapter Ten

Thursday and Friday were a giant blur. Between working on the final project that was due, and turning it in, and the two classes that had actual final exams to study for, I either lived at school or focused on school even when I came home. It didn't help any that I had two four-hour shifts at the Coffee Corner, but Maria needed the help. Most of the undergrad students who worked for her bailed to study and take finals.

Ben showed up at the apartment far earlier on Friday night than I had seen him on a weekend all semester.

Usually on Friday evenings he hung out with friends, maybe went out for pizza or a movie before coming home to dear old Mom.

This week, though, everybody must be in study mode. Since he'd gotten there so early I sprang for pizza for the two of us and we spent most of the evening with our various textbooks spread out in the living room. Ben commandeered the couch and I took over the armchair while we listened to music and studied. It was a strange and new thing to work on academic projects in the same room with my son without helping him with his homework. I figured some time during the weekend we might quiz each other on things. That would be even stranger than studying side by side.

Saturday morning found me in Dot's kitchen after kennel chores, having coffee and cinnamon rolls while we talked about our kids. I mentioned how odd it was to study with Ben like contemporaries. She nodded thoughtfully.

"I didn't have much of that with Candace, but we had our moments. She learned to sew in a class at school and we'd work on things together. Eventually she got tired of sewing and moved on to other things, but for a while we had fun. We even made a quilt together."

"Neat. Do you still have it?"

"She does. It's on her bed in Camarillo. Her 'real' bed, as she would say. We keep one bedroom set up for her here when she comes for a weekend, but our house doesn't feel like home to her anymore." Dot sipped her coffee. "But then I guess that's a good thing. That's what parenting is all about, raising kids to go off on their own as much as it's possible."

"Sure. That doesn't mean that it's all fun and games, though. I waver back and forth between missing the little boy I used to have and marveling at how much Ben reminds me of his dad, when I met him at college. Except that Ben's got more common sense."

Dot laughed. "Consider who raised him, my dear. What were Hal's parents like?"

"Wealthy. Divorced by the time he was in college, and both of them spoiled him rotten to get back at each other. If I'd looked critically at his parents, I might have thought twice about marrying their son. But at Ben's age while I may have had some common sense, I didn't have as much as he seems to have now."

"I'd like to meet your mother some time," Dot said. "Considering the way you turned out, she must be a pretty neat lady. Do you think she'll ever come out for a visit?"

"Maybe she will eventually. She actually likes the Midwestern winters, so it won't be anytime soon. She honestly doesn't understand why I don't want to go there for Christmas. Personally I feel like thirty-six white Christmases were enough, thank you."

Dot nodded. "If I wanted a white Christmas I'd go to Big Bear, where I can come back to decent weather in a day or two. Maybe we'll look better to her around February."

I shuddered. "Definitely. Even my mom can't love February in Missouri. That's the grayest twenty-eight days you can imagine."

"How do people live back there without sunshine? I don't know how I'd handle it, myself."

I wrapped my hands around my coffee mug. Just thinking about February in Missouri made me chilled. "If you're like me, you'd handle it poorly. You'd grouse a lot and dream of vacations someplace like this, and be very, very unhappy when you had to chop ice off your car for about the twelfth morning in a row."

"Not for me. I'll take California even if we have to put up with mudslides and earthquakes."

"So far I still think earthquakes are better than tornadoes. Especially since there aren't any basements to speak of out here. I can still remember sitting in the basement with Ben listening to the tornado sirens go off. At least that was back in the days when he felt safe just being with me. I'm afraid as your kids get older you just don't hold that power anymore."

"That's the truth. I think that not being able to keep her safe has been the hardest part of watching Candace grow up. When she was little I could fix most of the hurts, even when somebody teased her at school or she got sick. When she got older there was so much out there I couldn't protect her from anymore." Dot sighed. "But then, the hurts I couldn't fix started early with her because of the mistakes I made while I was carrying her."

I looked at Dot, and could tell that she was serious. "Surely you don't think that something you did while you were pregnant caused the Down syndrome?"

116

"No, not that. But I had a rough time the whole pregnancy and my doctor put me on something to keep me from miscarrying. It was years before we found out the drug he used was a bad idea."

"What was it?" The only problem drug like that I could think of was thalidomide, but that was before my time, much less Candace's, wasn't it?

"Have you ever heard of DES?" Dot clasped her hands on the table like a schoolmarm about to give a lesson. "But no, you probably haven't. Unless somebody you were close to had taken it, it wouldn't be an issue. It seemed to be a great drug at the time, but once those babies grew up a little there were all kinds of problems."

"You're right, it's one I haven't heard of," I told her. "What kinds of problems did it cause?"

"Reproductive issues, mostly. And for women there were increases in some kinds of cancer. Once we found out about the risks for Candace we were extra-careful about her having a yearly Pap test, even as a teenager. That was hard to explain to her."

"I imagine. How did she take it all?"

"Pretty well, considering." Dot paused for a moment. "We all handled it okay until one year her test was suspicious. She was put on an even more vigilant watch after that, and at nineteen she had surgery that removed the threat of cancer, but also left her unable to have children. That part of her problems I still feel that I could have changed if I'd only known."

"Maybe you could have." I patted her hand. Dot

117

looked more forlorn than I'd seen her before. She was usually one of the most upbeat people I knew. "But who's to say? We can't second-guess the past or the future."

"I know. It's all in God's hands anyway. And when we explained it all to her, Candace said it was okay with her because she didn't think she would make a good mommy anyway. It hardly ever comes up anymore."

"And she's stayed cancer-free since the surgery?"

"She has, so that's a blessing. All in all things could have been much worse. And there's part of me that knows that my guilt isn't really rational. I guess it's just that I'm a mom and I worry and I feel responsible for things like most of us do."

"I know what you mean there. I asked myself for years if I'd done the right thing not fighting the divorce when Hal and his parents were so adamant that it was the best thing for all of us. In hindsight, I think they just wanted him back in Tennessee. I was sure that the whole mess would leave Ben permanently scarred, even though he was so young when it happened that he hardly remembers a time when Hal and I lived together."

"Does he see his father very often?"

"They talk on the phone a lot. And for several weeks every summer he's there, as well as alternating holidays. This year he'll spend a good chunk of Christmas break with his father and grandparents and their various spouses." I didn't tell Dot that in all honesty I wished Ben spent more time with his father, but less with his father's scrapping, blended family. It wasn't the *blended* nature that bothered me, but the constant arguing. There never seemed to be a time when everyone was speaking to each other, and it made for some mighty contentious visits for Ben.

"So how do you feel about that? Is it hard to share him with them?" Even without me telling her the whole story, Dot seemed to know how I felt.

"It was a lot harder when he was younger. I wasn't happy about Ben flying alone, even as an unaccompanied minor on reliable airlines, until he was eleven or twelve. So there were quite a few uncomfortable meetings at midpoints between St. Louis and Memphis where Hal and I would be stiff and just barely civil to each other at some restaurant right off the highway as we traded Ben back and forth."

Dot shrugged. "At least you tried to be civil. I've seen too many cases where that didn't happen."

"Whatever other faults I found in Hal over the years, I have to say he put Ben first most of the time. After the divorce was final, that is." I shook my head to clear it. "But this is a pretty grim topic of conversation. Why don't we talk about something else?"

"That's a good idea. What are you going to bring to the Christian Friends holiday potluck next Sunday? I'm trying to decide between green bean casserole and broccoli salad."

I made a face. "I have to check with Linnette to see what I signed up for. I have no idea what kind of dish I'm supposed to bring." So the conversation drifted on to more pleasant things and eventually I drifted back to the apartment with a couple of cinnamon rolls that Dot sent with me for Ben.

Of course when I got back there I could hear Ben showering. It was after 10:30 in the morning, but before noon; a reasonable time to expect a college freshman to roll out of bed. After a short while—at least short for him as far as showers go—he came into the living room. Damp hair curled around his temples making him look boyish, but the Pac-Oaks hoodie and that awful goatee were both pure college man.

If the kid asks me what I want for Christmas, I'm tempted to tell him that a clean-shaven son would be wonderful. I can't imagine that happening until after the New Year begins, though. The only one who will be more aggravated by his facial hair than I am is Hal's mother, and unlike me, she will let Ben know frequently what she thinks of it all. I imagine he'll keep the goatee through the holidays just to vaguely aggravate his grandparents and give them a topic of conversation.

While Ben was still polishing off one of the cinnamon rolls and a cup of coffee as he studied, I heard a car door close outside. When I looked out there was a familiar unmarked sheriff's department vehicle in the driveway with Ray Fernandez standing outside. Of course, what would a Saturday morning be without a visit from the detective?

He went toward the front of the Morgans' house. I figured it was probably only a matter of time before he came back around this way. Sure enough, about twenty minutes later there was a knock on the door. I'd already warned my son that Fernandez was in the area, so Ben wasn't surprised when I opened the door and welcomed him in.

"I've got a fresh pot of coffee on. Would you like a cup?" I asked as soon as the pleasantries were over. "Ben, why don't you clear off half of the couch so that Detective Fernandez can sit down?"

"I'll take you up on the coffee, but don't pour me a full mug. I don't have time to visit today after I'm done asking the two of you a couple questions."

I noticed that Fernandez wasn't back to his "call me Ray" routine. Maybe we were back to formalities since he considered Ben a suspect in this murder. That was fine with me—I didn't really want to be on a first-name basis with anybody who thought my son was capable of something like that. I would, however, continue to offer him coffee. That's sort of like the "cup of cold water" we're supposed to offer folks, I figure.

I went in the kitchen and poured him the requested partial mug of coffee and brought it back into the living room. Fernandez was showing Ben a group of photographs. Ben shuffled through them, brow slightly wrinkled in thought.

"Yeah, definitely, that guy was here all the time. He was Frank's helper. He was usually here every day but Friday," Ben said, stopping at a picture of Darnell.

"Unless the surf was running just right somewhere between Santa Barbara and Malibu," I chimed in, putting down the coffee in front of Fernandez on the coffee table.

"That's already been pointed out to me," he said. "How about the guys in the other pictures?"

Ben flipped through the stack again. "These two I can't say for sure. Maybe Mom will have better luck telling you. But this guy, definitely. He wasn't here nearly as much as Darnell or anything. I think he worked with the plumbing crew."

Fernandez took the photos Ben handed him, holding them in such a way that I couldn't see which ones Ben indicated were parts of the crew or not. He shuffled them a little and passed them to me. I sat down in the armchair next to his end of the couch. "What is this all about?" I thought I knew, but it was better to have things clarified.

"I wanted to show you and Ben some pictures to see if you recognized some of the young men that we've identified as part of the construction crews. All of the people I'm showing you worked for one contractor or another, but not all of them necessarily worked on this job. Mrs. Morgan was very helpful, but as the actual tenant of the apartment, you might be able to add details."

He took a sip of his coffee and looked at me while I began to study the pictures. Those golden brown eyes could certainly focus with an intensity that made me antsy. I tried to get my attention on the photos instead of the man watching me. I looked through them, reordering the group. The first two were easy. "Ben's

122

right, Darnell was here all the time. And if this second guy was here at all, I don't remember him." I handed back those two photos.

The other two were more problematic. "I have to admit that I'm not sure how often I saw this young man on the job here, but I know who he is. I met him at the funeral home during Frank's visitation, and I'm pretty sure that I'd seen Bob Leopold around here on at least one occasion with his dad's plumbing crew."

Fernandez looked at me over the rim of his coffee cup. "Okay. Fair enough," he said, putting it down. "What about the fourth one?"

I studied the remaining photo. The young man was incredibly ordinary looking, with brown hair and a thin sort of face. His eyes looking out at the camera seemed to be focusing on a point in the distance and he wasn't smiling. He could have been any one of a dozen kids that came through the Coffee Corner on a daily basis *or* were part of one of the construction crews. "Honestly, he looks familiar but I can't tell you exactly why. I couldn't tell you that he was definitely working on the apartment, Detective, because I'm not sure where I've seen him before."

"But you have seen him?" That golden intensity was back in his gaze.

"I think I have. Like I said, though, I couldn't tell you where. Between the Coffee Corner, Ben's dorm and the ongoing parade of workers who've come through here on the remodeling job, I see a lot of young men in their late teens and early twenties."

"That's okay, Ms. Harris. All I wanted was for you to give it your best shot. Your answers don't have to please me. They just have to be the truth." He stood to leave and I stood with him.

"Does this mean you're focusing on people other than Ben in your investigation now?" Ben gave me a look behind Fernandez's back that seemed to tell me to sit down and shut up. I cheerfully ignored him.

"We are, to tell you the truth. Of course we still can't rule anyone out at this stage of the game. However there are several individuals I need to talk to whose prints have shown up where Ben's didn't. Or yours, either, for that matter."

"Well, I'm glad to hear that." Had he really considered me a suspect at any time? I couldn't imagine it, but with Fernandez it was hard to tell. "I mean, I'm glad my prints didn't show up anyplace strange, not that you're considering the young men on the construction crew. I imagine most of them have mothers who will be just as upset as I am to know their sons are suspects in a murder."

"Probably so. Somewhere out there is one mother who won't be at all surprised when we come knocking on her door. Few murders happen out of the blue."

Fernandez's words made me shiver. What would it be like to think someone as close to you as your son was capable of murder? It was difficult for me to imagine.

"How much chance do you have of solving this one? I've always heard that homicides that aren't solved in the first few days are less likely to be solved at all."

Fernandez pointed a finger at me. "You've been watching those cop shows on TV again, haven't you? That's not necessarily so. Some crimes, like gang shootings, usually need a witness who's willing to talk or something else that has to come up quickly. But a lot of the rest are solved by good old-fashioned police work and sometimes that takes time."

He gave me another look on his way out that told me that when it came to solving this murder, Ray Fernandez would take all the time he needed. Once more I was glad that Ben no longer seemed to be his primary suspect.

Chapter Eleven

Sunday began quietly. I got up and read my passages for women's Bible study class, which I should have done days ago but hadn't. I savored a couple cups of hot coffee while I read, waiting for Ben to get up. He'd told me the night before that he would go to church with me if I didn't go to the earliest service possible.

I had showered the night before, so we didn't have any squabbles over the hot water when he finally got up, about half an hour later than I would have to make it to church at 9:30 a.m. Still, he managed to be ready only five minutes after I was hoping to leave. When we got to the Chapel he actually found a couple of other Pacific Oaks students to hang out with while I went to my Bible class.

I sat with the usual suspects in Sunday school. Most

of them belonged to Christian Friends. I was a little surprised to see Tracy Collins slip into the room just before class started. If she saw Dot motion for her to come sit by us, she ignored it. Instead she slid into an empty chair in the back of the room. I don't think she said a word the entire hour, but she was there and I hoped she'd gotten something out of the class. If anybody could use the comfort of Scripture right now it had to be Tracy.

She was still in the room when class broke up, and Dot went over to say hello. I followed her, not sure whether I should say anything or not. I didn't have to worry; Dot did most of the talking and I was free to stand there and keep them company.

"I guess you've heard the latest," Tracy told her. "The police say Frank was definitely shot with one of his own guns. I told him more than once he shouldn't keep that thing in the cab of the truck. But my advice wasn't something he listened to on anything else. Why should this have been different?" There were circles under her eyes dark as bruises. I wondered if she'd slept since the funeral.

"I knew that much," Dot admitted. "That detective working the case, Ray Fernandez, has been out to ask me questions more than once. He was at the house yesterday to show me pictures and have me see if I knew any of the men in them. Apparently most of them were on one or another of the crews that worked with Frank."

"Yeah, that same detective told me they were trying to narrow down suspects because there were other prints on the gun besides Frank's. But I told him what I've been telling everybody else, that there were so many people that Frank owed money to or had cheated one way or another in business that I could give him the names of about fifteen suspects."

Dot's eyebrows raised. "That many? How?"

Tracy's shoulders sagged. "It's like a broken record on the phone messages, with people telling me how much money they need from me by next week. And Frank's books are so sloppy I can't tell what he really paid anybody and what he was trying to lie his way out of paying. How we will keep the house is going to be anybody's guess."

Dot patted her on the shoulder. "You know, we've got several people here at the Chapel who are good accountants. They offer their services to members in trouble sometimes. I'd say you definitely qualify. Maybe you could call Pastor George and ask him to link you up with somebody."

Tracy seemed to perk up for the first time. "That sounds like a good idea. I can't afford to pay a good accountant, or even a mediocre one. Even though I've done lots of bookkeeping this mess is beyond me. There are so many other things to sort through and settle that I could spend all my time on other problems anyway."

"Besides the bookkeeping, what's the worst of your worries? I'll check tonight with my Christian Friends group. Maybe we could help you out." I almost nudged Dot in the ribs to tell her not to get us involved in more than we could handle. But then, considering what the Christian Friends had done for me, and for Heather, maybe they could handle just about anything.

Tracy sighed again. "Probably the worst of it otherwise is Frankie. He's staying out until all hours and I know he's cutting classes during the daytime. At thirteen he won't listen to me, and when he does come home he spends all his time at his computer. I know this is hard for him to handle, but I don't need more problems right now on top of what I've got."

"I hate to sound sexist, but this sounds more like a job for a man, maybe. Do you think Frankie could handle some of the chores around the kennels at our place? I know Buck could use a hand, and he's willing to pay for the help. It might give Frankie some incentive to shape up." Dot smiled faintly. "I know if he works at the kennels very long it will tire him out enough that he won't have much energy to stay out late."

Tracy's answering smile was even fainter than Dot's, but it was there nonetheless. "I'll work on him. It might not sound good to him at first, but he knows we could use the money. Even if I let him keep everything he earned it would probably come in handy because I wouldn't have to give him money for school and things he thinks he has to have. Thanks, Dot."

"Anything that I can do to help I will. I'll let Buck know what I've gotten him into so he will be ready to talk to Frankie." They chatted a little while longer about the best times during the week for Tracy to bring her son over, and I drifted toward the door to avoid eavesdropping on any more of their private conversation.

Dot caught up with me a few minutes later near the coffee urn in the fellowship hall. "Sorry if I seem to be giving away some of your hours around the kennel, but I figured you wouldn't mind terribly."

"Especially not for the next week while I've got finals," I told her. "Besides, I know Tracy could use the help with Frankie, and the money, far more than I need it."

"You're right there. I know you need it, too, Gracie Lee, but I figure one of these days Dennis's probate case will work its way through the courts and maybe you'll get back what he owed you."

I shrugged my shoulders. "To tell you the truth, Dot, it's not something I'm counting on anytime soon. Someday, perhaps. It would certainly provide more of a cushion for me and for Ben while I finish school."

"True. But even if we cut your hours around the kennel, you know that you'll have cheap rent as long as you need it."

I was so touched by Dot's words I teared up a little. Making a go of it as a single mom has never been easy, and right now with a limited income and not much to fall back on, it's more of a challenge than ever. I'd gotten Dennis's insurance company to settle a portion of his small life insurance policy. He'd named his mom as beneficiary, but then she died shortly after he did. With Lexy's help as an attorney, I'd convinced the insurance company that I was entitled to some of the proceeds of that policy. Right now that money was about all I had to fall back on when I needed it.

Getting the thirty thousand dollars that Dennis had bilked me out of would be enough to tide me over without worries until I finished my degree and got a counseling position somewhere. But so far I'd done all right trusting that God would keep things together. I knew it would be fine as long as I didn't make any stupid decisions. I could hardly believe that Dot and Buck cutting my hours back a little each week was against God's plan if it helped Tracy and her family.

Before I could think about it all anymore, Ben stood next to me in the fellowship hall. "Come on, Mom. I want to get into services while the praise band is still playing. They're really good and I want to listen a while," he said with more enthusiasm than I expected. I wondered if that meant there were cute girls in the praise band. I guess that makes me a cynical mom, but he's been a teenager long enough for me to understand his motives far more often than I'd like.

By the time evening rolled around and it was time for my Christian Friends meeting again I was plenty ready for the friendly adult companionship. Ben had studied all afternoon, and instead of joining him I'd gotten called in for a shift at work.

Fernandez hadn't called or come over today; I didn't know whether to think that was a good thing or a bad thing. He wasn't asking Ben or me questions right now, but he hadn't made any other big announcements that I'd heard, either.

After filling in for another server all afternoon, I went straight to Conejo Community Chapel alone. I'd gotten used to a different routine all summer when I was only taking one class and working shorter hours at the coffeeshop. Then Dot and I had driven to meetings together most of the time. Now it seemed like I drove around in the dark alone a lot. California might not be cold in the winter, but this area got dark just as early in the evening, or almost afternoon, as the Midwest did in December.

At least this time I wasn't coming empty-handed to the meeting. Once Maria found out where I was going, she insisted that I take an insulated-air pot full of fresh-brewed decaf with me. I certainly didn't argue with her, since I almost never took a turn at bringing anything for the snack tray. I'd caught Linnette via cell phone and told her not to make coffee.

Now I trudged through the church parking lot, noticing that one of the lights had burned out. It left a large corner of the parking area in the dark. Given the number of coyotes and even mountain lions sighted around the area I could have done without more shadows. I felt relief when I got to the door and went in.

The well-lit church hallway felt much safer than outside. Rational thought told me I was too big, tough and stringy to be coyote bait, but telling myself that didn't do anything to calm my overactive imagination in the dark. Being inside with lights around me was reassuring. Given the time I knew the group started without me, so I sped up to get into the room.

As I expected, folks were already filling small plates with cookies and looking hopefully at the door for coffee to go with them. Paula waved and motioned me over to where things were set up. "Finally, the coffee lady. And there's somebody here waiting especially for you." She turned and tapped another woman on the shoulder. "Tracy, you said to tell you when Gracie Lee got here."

"Yeah, I did," Tracy Collins said, turning toward me. In a split second all my feelings of safety evaporated as she charged past a surprised Paula and gave me a push to both shoulders that had me sitting on my posterior on the carpet, seeing a few stars. Maybe, I thought, I should have taken my chances with the coyotes instead of coming inside.

Needless to say, mass chaos erupted then. Voices were raised while Paula just stood there looking stunned. Dot and Linnette took charge of Tracy while Lexy got me up and as far away from the others as possible. Heather, who had been sitting in a chair with a blanket pulled over her and Corinna, stayed rooted to that spot, wide-eyed. In a moment there was a thin wail under the blanket where the baby obviously felt neglected. I felt like wailing along with her.

Dot and Linnette marched Tracy over to me a few minutes later. "We don't tolerate verbal or physical attacks on anybody in this group," Linnette said sternly as she looked at Tracy. "I know Paula invited you here and as such probably should be responsible for you, but she didn't know the whole situation. If you want to stay, you need to make things right with Gracie Lee."

Tracy started to sputter. "*Me* make things right with *her*? She's the one who has come right up to me twice to talk to me about Frank and never told me that her own son was a suspect in his murder!" She glared at me. "You were just pumping me for information to try and get your kid off the hook."

At least now I had an idea why she pushed me. "That's not true. I've been through some of what you have and I actually wanted to help if I could," I told her. Right now I felt very sorry that I'd ever tried to offer her any sympathy. "My husband was murdered last winter. It was a hard time for me, even though I didn't have little kids depending on me for support."

Tracy deflated a little. She shot a subtle glance at Paula and then looked back at me. "Nobody told me that. I'm sorry I pushed you. My emotions ran away with me. Maybe I really just want somebody to blame for some of the rotten stuff that's happened to us."

"Well, I'm not the person to blame. Ben isn't, either. Detective Fernandez has as good as said that my son isn't a suspect in Frank's murder anymore."

"I wish he'd give me some idea who *is* a suspect, then." Tracy's eyes filled with tears. "I have enough problems right now without worrying about whether the rest of us are safe. Frankie keeps asking me if whoever killed his dad is going to come to the house. He's sleeping with a baseball bat."

"That's a terrible worry for a thirteen-year-old. You ought to tell Ray Fernandez about it. Maybe he could talk to Frankie and reassure him nobody's out to hurt any of you." My emotions were on a seesaw tonight. I'd gone from feeling fear and anger back to sympathy for Tracy Collins again in less than half an hour.

"Until you can do that tomorrow, you can always talk about it all here with us," Linnette said from behind Tracy. "And we can pray about our troubles. Now how about we get this meeting started the way it's supposed to run? Everybody find a seat and get comfortable."

"Certainly," Paula piped up. "I'll get settled as soon as I get some coffee. Unless Gracie Lee spilled it all in the commotion."

I could see Dot shaking her head, eyes rolled toward the ceiling. Leave it to Paula to get totally worked up about a side issue. This was going to be a long evening.

Everybody got coffee and I grabbed a brownie from the goodies set out. We all found a seat without any other disasters and even Corinna settled back down and slept in Heather's arms. It would be nice to be that easy to calm down. A little warm milk, a pat or two on the back and the baby was happy.

Linnette led us in prayer and a short devotion before opening up the floor to those who wanted to talk. As the newcomer Tracy went first. There were a few tears as she told her story. Not all of them were hers.

When she finished Dot raised a hand. "Go on," Linnette told her. "You look like you have something to add."

"I do." Dot looked serious again. The last two weeks had taken a toll on my normally-cheerful landlady.

Tonight she almost looked like the 71-year-old woman she was.

"Tracy, you said earlier that you were anxious to have more information about Frank's murder. I may be able to tell you something in a few days. Detective Fernandez called me this afternoon while I was getting ready to come here. He wants to meet me at the group home where Candace lives tomorrow morning."

"What for?" Tracy looked puzzled. "She wasn't anywhere near your house when this happened, was she?"

"No, she wasn't. But the detective has questions for her anyway. He wants to talk to her and her roommate Lucy Perez, and he wants me present as well as Lucy's sister Estella, her guardian. He has some reason to want to talk to the two of them and I certainly intend to be there."

The rest of the Christian Friends might not know all the connections between Frank Collins and Candace that made Ray want to question her and her roommate. But I was sure it was going to be a difficult morning for Dot and her daughter. And depending on what her answers to the detective's questions were, I was afraid it might be a bad day for Matt afterward.

Chapter Twelve

There was no good reason for me to tag along to the group home in the morning. I really wanted to, just to see what Ray Fernandez was going to ask Candace and Lucy. In the end, however, I exercised good judgment and stayed home while Dot and Buck drove over to Camarillo. Once Buck heard about the need for Candace to be interviewed he insisted on going along. It made me feel more at ease to know Candace would have plenty of protection.

Not that she'd need that much protection. I had to admit that Ray was usually tough but fair in his investigations and followed the law to the letter. Since Candace had done absolutely nothing wrong, she wouldn't have any problems with the detective.

As Dot and Buck drove away I finished up the kennel work by myself. Doing all of it for them this morning meant that Buck could take a shower and dress to go with Dot in the time he would have spent feeding dogs. He'd argued with me at first, but I felt it was the least I could do and told him so. In the end he got ready and I cleaned out kennels and fed dogs. The census was relatively low anyway; all the pups had gone to new homes already and a cold snap had moved Dixie, Sophie and Hondo inside.

When the kennel chores were finished I actually went out and spent money on something that wasn't a necessity. That was a rare thing for me right now, but this year I wasn't going to do without a Christmas tree of my own. Even with the limited space in the apartment I wanted this December to be special.

It would technically be my first Christmas without Dennis. Technically because last year he'd been comatose at the Conejo Board and Care this time of year. I'd gone there often in December and sat by his

136

bedside. The piped-in Christmas carols in the facility sounded dreary, and the decorations looked tired. This year would be a time for my own CDs of upbeat songs and true rejoicing during the season.

Even though I don't have a clue where it's going to get stored in January, I bought an artificial tree. Real trees smell wonderful, but it always makes me sad to think of killing a tree just for a few weeks of it sitting in my living room. Besides, if I am going to keep having Sophie or one of the other dogs in here for company, an artificial tree will be much smarter. I can still remember learning new words when I was six from what my dad said when Buttons the puppy knocked over the tree trying to drink out of the water well of the tree stand. Dogs and a real tree inside the house just aren't a good mix.

By the time the Morgans got back home I'd lugged the tree home from the discount store and set it up in the corner of my living room. Splurging on one with lights wired on turned out to be a good thing, because there were no working lights in the one box of Christmas decorations I'd carted around since the move from Missouri. The box hadn't been opened since I moved it, because I'd spent last Christmas at Edna's house. She hadn't even considered sharing her Christmas tree for any of my decorations.

I heard Buck's car pull into the garage beneath the apartment as I sorted through ornaments. It was funny to look at things like the preschool treasures from Ben's younger years. I especially like the ornament made from an orange juice can lid with rickrack glued around the edge.

Hanging that one on the tree, I left the rest of the box and went outside to see how the morning had gone at the group home. "Come over and have lunch," Dot called from the driveway. "I put soup in the slow-cooker to warm up before we left. And I want to tell you what went on."

"Sure." No sense in turning down a great offer. Food and information are my favorite combination. If Dot had any Christmas cookies baked for dessert, lunch would be perfect.

I went back inside to grab a sweater and my purse so that I could lock up the apartment. Even when I'm only across the way at the "big house" I don't like leaving things unlocked without anybody there. Rancho Conejo nearly always makes the "ten safest cities in America" list for places its size, but I still lock my door. I figure it's one less way to lead somebody into temptation if they're prone to thievery.

There were three places set at Dot's kitchen table, each with a cheery red-and-green placemat, crockery soup bowl, matching mug and a dog on the floor beside the chair. I don't think the dogs were supposed to be part of the décor.

"This is your fault," she said to Buck as she brandished a soup ladle. "If you didn't feed Hondo from the table none of them would expect anything."

Buck shrugged and sat down at his place. Once settled he gave a command to the dogs that at least made all of them lie down and stop begging, although there was a tail thump once in a while. Dot filled the soup bowls and reached over to take my hand so that Buck could say grace. I liked the tradition of table prayers with everybody holding hands. It's a little late to start with Ben but I still may give it a shot.

"Heavenly Father," Buck began, "we want to thank You for this food and ask You to use it to strengthen our bodies to Your service. Please guide us in what we say and do today, and be with Candace and Lucy and their friends as they go about the rest of their day. Thank You for upholding them and helping them tell the truth this morning, and give the sheriff's department people discernment to sort out the right information. In Jesus's name we pray. Amen." We echoed the amen and Dot gave my hand a squeeze.

Her soup was delicious and I told her so once I'd had a few bites. "So how did things go this morning?" I tried to be as casual as possible, but I'm sure Dot could see I was champing at the bit for information.

"I think they went well, wouldn't you say so, Buck?" He nodded in answer to the question and kept eating his soup. "Detective Fernandez was there when we arrived, but he didn't go inside the house until we went in with him. Lucy's sister couldn't make it, but she'd authorized Kirsten to be Lucy's advocate if she needed one."

"Was that okay with the detective?" I wondered if he felt he could still proceed, or if it changed his interview any. Neither question was one I was likely to get an answer to from Ray, even if I'd asked him point-blank.

"He said it was the best he was going to get," Buck said. "Then he went on and asked his questions while we all sat around their dining room table. Candace and Lucy seemed at ease that way. Not much that he asked them seemed out of the ordinary. Mostly he just wanted to know how they knew Frank, and what kind of contact they'd had with him."

"How much contact was there?" I figured there would be two answers to this one.

"More than I would have thought," Dot interjected. "I knew what Candace would say. She still remembers Frank from when he did the renovations on her apartment out back the first time. She didn't much like him then, and she didn't grow any fonder of him recently."

"What about Lucy? Overhearing her and Matt at the funeral, it sounded as if she knew Frank."

"She did. I knew he'd gone into the restaurant where Candace works once in a while, mainly because it's a buffet and it's inexpensive." Dot frowned. "What I didn't know is that he seemed to have taken to visiting the movie theater in the same shopping center, where Lucy works. He must have made a pest of himself from what she said."

"That's putting it nicely," Buck said. "Your cousin was always a hound where young women were concerned. No offense to present company." He spoke the last bit down at Hondo, who whined softly.

Dot shook her head. "If it had been someone else they were talking about, I would have thought that the girls saying that Frank took them out for ice cream after work and dropped them off at the group home was perfectly innocent. But with him involved I would look twice at his motives."

"Hopefully Detective Fernandez will, too. I'd hate to think Frank was trying to prey on somebody as defenseless as Lucy."

Buck got up and got himself another bowl of soup, then sat down heavily at his place at the table, looking serious. "He may have done more than try, Gracie Lee. The one thing that Lucy said that was the most disturbing was that Frank hit on her, and that was why Matt hit him back."

"Wow. I guess we know where the detective went after he talked to the girls." When Buck refilled his bowl more soup sounded good. Now I'd lost my appetite. I didn't want anybody else going through the kind of suspicion that Ben had, or even worse. But it sounded like things were about to get tough for Matt Seavers.

Dwelling on Matt and what happened to him was something I put aside for a while that day. At four I went back to school to take my final. When I came home from school I discovered that Sam Blankenship left a message on my answering machine. His message asked five or six more detailed questions about the investigation into Frank's death. In the background while he talked I could hear rattling sounds that might have been a potato chip bag. Apparently junior reporters on the newspaper still didn't make enough money to go out for lunch.

On the phone Sam sounded a little more seasoned now. I may have helped that seasoning process a little by insisting that he be the one to cover the story once we knew who'd killed Dennis. He'd been helpful and pleasant up to that point and I'd felt I owed him one. I couldn't take credit for much, though. Most of his growth probably came from just covering the stories he needed to cover in nine months. His byline climbed up the ladder a few rungs in that time so that by now he wasn't just covering three-alarm fires and suspicious deaths at nursing homes.

Listening to his message I decided that the reporter must not be any friendlier with Fernandez. The detective could have answered any of the questions Sam asked me, but he'd chosen to ask me about the details of Frank's death and what had happened in the two weeks since.

I called Tuesday morning to talk to Sam but only got his voice mail. Either some story broke that they needed him to cover or he still wasn't much of a morning person. Given that he was hardly older than Ben, that didn't surprise me much. We might play telephone tag for another day or two, given my schedule. After returning his call I put in a shift at the Coffee Corner and took my last final.

When I finished and went home, Ben drove up to the apartment and proceeded to unload his car as I got out of mine. It took quite a while to help him unload, and involved three trips up and down the stairs for each of us.

"Are you sure you need all this stuff over winter break?" I asked him as I huffed and puffed under a comforter piled on top of a laundry basket.

"Yeah, most of it. I can't go back into the dorm after today until the tenth of January when next semester starts. That means I had to pack up anything I wanted to use in the next month, and anything I was afraid might get stolen if somebody broke into the suite." That apparently encompassed virtually everything he owned. I felt thankful the microwave and refrigerator that he and Ted shared didn't get hauled to the apartment.

With what he brought home his bedroom soon looked like a war zone. It felt like his early high school years when I was always haranguing him to clean up his stuff. Given the lack of closet space in the apartment and the unfinished nature of the bathroom at this point, I wasn't even going to bother to nag. As long as he kept most of it in his bedroom where he could close the door, I could live with the clutter for a month. It felt so good to have him home. I'd missed him even though he had spent a lot of weekends here with me.

After an hour or so of things moving around behind the closed bedroom door, Ben opened it and came out. He had changed into his usual baggy shorts and a hoodie and looked very comfortable. "Now that you're here does this mean I'm cooking supper for two?"

He looked a little sheepish. "Not tonight. There's a bunch of people going out to celebrate the end of the semester. I want to have a little bit more time with some of them before they take off for home."

"Okay. Maybe tomorrow night, then." Having a teenager had made me fairly flexible. With Ben, plans were always in flux until the last moment.

Ben grimaced. "Maybe Thursday? There's a movie opening tomorrow I promised a friend I'd see with her."

Hmm. This was a new development. I fairly burst keeping more questions to myself. The first mention of a female friend to see movies with wasn't the time to grill him on their relationship. If this mystery woman was more than a casual friend, I'd start hearing her name soon enough. That or see her number show up on the cell phone bill. I made a mental note to look more carefully when the bill came this month.

"Okay." I hugged him, marveling at the maturity and height my kid had gained. "Drive carefully, make everybody wear their seat belts—"

"And nobody smokes in the car and call you if I'm going to be later than one," he finished up. This wasn't a new litany of requests. So far he nearly always remembered them. I didn't have to add a caution about drinking because I knew Ben didn't drink. Lots of freshmen celebrated their independence that way, but we already had more than one conversation about alcohol since he'd come to California in June.

We'd had an ongoing series of conversations about drinking from middle school on up, and Ben's answer was always the same. He thought it was stupid, much to my delight. There's a lot to be thankful for in having a stubborn kid. It makes reasoning with them difficult from the time they learn to talk, but it also has its pluses in the teen years. Few of their peers can sway them into bad behavior if they aren't prone to it in the first place.

Ben left and I got back to decorating the tree. By the time my stomach started reminding me I was hungry I was alone in an apartment lit only by the glow of the tree lights I'd plugged in. It felt peaceful to sit there that way, not needing to study for a change or go into work. I decided to have a real treat and go over to my favorite place for fish tacos and actually stay there and eat at a table for a change. Normally I got carryout and ate it at home, but tonight I wanted to have some contact with other grown-ups.

The atmosphere at the small mom-and-pop restaurant about two miles from the apartment was festive. It was warm inside and strung with Christmas garland, white lights and bright decorations. There was a sign behind the cash register that said they were taking orders for tamales for Christmas. That was a tradition I hadn't gotten into yet although I knew a lot of Californians even made their own. I wasn't about to do that for two people. From what I understood it was a massive undertaking best suited to having a family's worth of women and a large kitchen.

I ordered a fish taco platter with black beans and rice and sat down at a table to wait for my food. I'd brought the newspaper to read, celebrating the luxury of not having to read stuff for class. My back was to the door of the restaurant so between newspaper sections I could watch the work in the open kitchen. I like restaurants where you can see into the food prep area. It's the quickest way to judge the quality and cleanliness of a place. More than once since moving here I've wondered why Ventura County doesn't follow its neighbor LA County in having grade stickers in the windows of restaurants. I like that big blue "A" reassuring me.

Still, this place, called *Mi Familia*, didn't give me any cause for worry. The spotless nature of their open kitchen, added to the fact they made the best fish tacos around, made it my favorite place to eat besides my own kitchen. As I watched the small staff as they bustled around the kitchen and in front, I heard the bell on the door ring, signaling another customer.

The dark-haired man who went up to the counter looked familiar. His jeans and windbreaker didn't help me recognize him, although I liked the view from the back. Then Luis behind the counter said, "*Señor* Ray, your order is almost ready," and it dawned on me who I was looking at. Ray Fernandez looked different somehow without a suit jacket. He seemed more relaxed, too.

I was still figuring out how much to say to him when he took the cup Luis handed him and turned to fill it at the soda machine. He did a mild double take when he saw me, and walked over to my table without filling his cup. "Hi. How's it going?"

All kinds of snappy answers raced through my mind, such as, *It would be going just great if you could reassure me that Ben isn't a suspect in your murder investigation,* but I rejected all of them. "Okay. Are you off duty?" The minute the question was out I wanted to take it back.

"Yeah, I am. Picking up a late dinner on the way home. You enjoying an after-dinner rest or waiting for food?"

He was smiling for a change, but the man looked tired. I debated silently for a minute and then followed an internal urging that had to be from the Lord because I sure wasn't bold enough to do it myself.

"Waiting for food. If I promise not to bring up the case on my own, do you want to join me? Personally I couldn't stand another night in that apartment alone for dinner."

The smile broadened, making the skin around his eyes crinkle in a way that made him look approachable in a way I've never seen Ray Fernandez look. "I might even bring the case up in general terms myself. I need somebody to bounce some stuff off of who isn't in the department or a lawyer." He called out something in Spanish to Luis, who nodded. Then Ray walked around the table to the chair next to me. "All right if I sit here?"

"Sure. Any of the three empty chairs are fine." I'd figured he would sit across from me, creating as much space between us as possible, but that wasn't happening.

He must have seen my questioning look, because he laughed. "It's a cop thing. I can't sit with my back to that counter, or to the door, either. It has to be the seat closest to a wall, facing out so I can see the whole restaurant."

I'd never considered seat placement quite that way before, but seen from his perspective it made sense. "All right. Wherever you feel comfortable is fine by me."

My taco platter came soon after he settled in. "Please, go ahead and eat while it's hot. Don't wait for me and let it get cold," he urged.

I debated on what to do. Cold fish tacos weren't wonderful, but I felt a little odd eating in front of him. Still, it would only take a couple more minutes for his food to get here. While I waited, I decided to say grace over my food silently. Ray started to say something to me and then stopped himself short. When it became clear I had finished, he kept looking at me, those golden brown eyes looking mystified. "You really do that? Pray over your food in a restaurant?"

"Yep. I really do that. Hope it doesn't make you uncomfortable, but if it does I have to tell you that it's too bad because I won't stop doing it for your sake."

He gave a short laugh. "That's what I like about you, Gracie Lee. You're never afraid to say what's on your mind."

"That I'm not. So why don't you tell me whatever it is you want to bounce off somebody while I start on a fish taco?"

"Sure. First of all, I have to tell you that Ben is pretty much out of the running as a suspect. Now that I've talked to Matt Seavers, it's pretty clear that he was the person the Morgans saw talking to Frank Collins."

I sagged visibly with relief. This was a better early

Christmas present than having Ben shave. "Thank you." My words were half addressed to Ray and half to God.

Ray smiled again. "I knew you'd be glad to hear that. What you won't be glad to hear is that I want to hold Seavers for questioning. I gather from Mrs. Morgan that you and your church friends are sure he had nothing to do with this murder."

"You're right there. I haven't met the kid yet, but from the things Dot has said, it's hard to imagine he's a murderer."

"Maybe so, for you. I've seen a lot stranger killers, I can tell you. And the bottom line is there's something wrong with his story."

"Maybe so, but does that add up to murder?"

Ray shrugged, the light fading from his eyes. "For a change, I'm not sure. When you finish eating I want to walk you through everything that happened that morning and see if it gives me a different perspective."

"I'll be happy to do that." I was willing to do anything that might make him rethink Candace's friend as a murder suspect. Luis came bearing Ray's hot plate and we both settled down to eating in silence. While this was far from a date, it felt decidedly odd to be eating dinner in Ray's company. I was silently praying again, but this time it was for something very concrete: I prayed that I wouldn't make a fool of myself picking up drippy fish tacos in front of somebody who seemed to value my opinion. It was a small thing but if we're to trust God in everything, I figured He could handle one drippy fish taco.

Chapter Thirteen

We were both fast eaters, so dinner was a memory in a short time. Then Fernandez surprised me even more. "Have you ever tried the flan here? Luis's wife makes it from her mom's recipe and it's great. How about I buy us dessert?"

Could we actually have something in common, even if it was a simple thing like a love of good desserts? I'd never considered that before but it was intriguing. "Sure. I've got nowhere else to go and you seem to want to talk some more."

He laughed again, a rich deep sound I could get used to hearing. When had the pod people visited the Ventura County sheriff station and replaced one detective? "I consider myself hard to read. I'm trained to have a poker face. Why am I that obvious to you?"

"I don't know. Maybe because you make me uncomfortable and I am usually trying not to tick you off."

His face fell. "Aw, seriously? I was hoping it was because you were fascinated by my good looks."

Was he *flirting* with me? Even if he wasn't, this was a light and candid side of Ray I hadn't seen before. I liked it but I had no idea what brought it on. "Well that, too, but I'm afraid it's mostly because you make me feel like I'm back in high school and about to get detention."

He shrugged. "I do have that effect sometimes. With some people, like that reporter from the *Star*, it doesn't bother me. I guess it's just the breaks of the game with this job. You want coffee to go with that flan?"

"Make it decaf and you've got a deal." He went up to the counter and a few minutes later came back with our coffee and dessert. I was glad to see that he had two plates on the tray. It would have felt way too much like a date if he'd brought back one plate and two spoons. I wasn't about to go that far with my friendly neighborhood detective yet. Perhaps there could come a day when I'd consider dating again, but this wasn't the day.

"You're right about the flan. It's great," I told him after two bites. Why did he have to be right so often on so many things? "So what is it about Matt that makes you uncomfortable or uneasy?"

Fernandez gave a short bark of laughter. "Now see, that's the thing. He doesn't make me uneasy. That's what I don't get."

"I'll have to admit you lost me. If Matt doesn't worry you, why are you thinking of arresting him?"

Ray steepled his hands, fingers and thumbs forming a triangle while he framed thoughts as well. If this guy wasn't a homicide detective he'd make a great college lecturer. "Normally I don't believe anybody. Or almost anybody. That's because most people lie to me."

"And you expect them to," I put in. Maybe that was a little bold, but it was implied in what he said.

"Yes, I do. A lot of people feel they have good reason to lie in answer to the questions I ask during an investigation. Some have the best reason of all . . . if they told the truth I'd arrest them on the spot."

151

The light was beginning to dawn on me. "But Matt worries you because he seems to be telling the truth?"

"Yeah, I think so. There's something a little off about his story and I can't figure out exactly what that is. But for the most part I think he's telling me the truth and I don't understand it."

"Why? What would you expect him to lie about?"

"Lots of things. We found his prints on the murder weapon, but not where I expect to find a murderer's print. That doesn't completely rule him out, because there's nothing usable on the trigger of the gun. Seavers's prints are on the barrel, and he volunteered right away how they got there."

I took a sip of coffee while it was still hot enough to enjoy. "Which is how, if you can tell me?"

"Matt claims he and Collins got into a sparring match, verbal at first, and then physical, over the way Collins treated Lucy."

"Candace's roommate who is also Matt's girlfriend," I put in. "And that would explain the scraped knuckles he had as well, so he didn't try to lie his way out of that, either."

"No, and he could have. Working in construction like he does, Matt could have given me half a dozen reasons why his hands looked that way."

"So you want to arrest him for telling the truth because it sounds funny to you?"

Ray shrugged. "My reasons sound dumb when you put it that way. He may be truthful but there's something Matt's leaving out or glossing over. If he didn't kill Collins then he's the last person to see him alive besides the killer. Matt claims he fought with Collins but that when he left, the guy was alive, basically in one piece and on the pavement near his own truck."

"And that certainly wasn't where I found him."

"Exactly. Added to the fact that Matt has no driver's license, it doesn't add up to the whole truth."

I shook my head. "You lost me again. How does that figure into the equation?"

"He had to get to the construction site at the Morgans' somehow. Either somebody drove him there or he's driving without a license. In the first case he could be an accessory to murder if whoever drove him there killed Collins. If he drove himself I've got something to hold him on for a while until I figure out what else is bugging me."

"Couldn't it be more innocent than that? Does the kid have any family who would drive him places?"

"Not that I've found so far. His mom is out of the picture, has been for years. His dad is an alcoholic who lost his license years ago on repeat DWIs, so if either of them is driving a car it's a big problem."

"How does Matt get around for work if he doesn't drive? I know the bus service in this end of the county isn't all that great." I'd tried to use it myself at times to save the outrageous cost of gas, but it turned out to be more hassle than it was worth.

"I still have to check that out. Once he's on the job with Leopold it's not a problem because he never works alone. Somebody else is always there supervising and drives the truck."

"This is all getting pretty circular for me. No matter what you've got on Matt, it doesn't sound like you have enough to arrest him."

"Not for murder. But he's hiding something and until I figure out what it is, I can't trust everything he says."

"So where does that leave you? There's not enough evidence to charge him with anything, but you still have that nagging feeling—dare I say intuition—that something is wrong."

"Exactly. Although I wouldn't call it intuition." Of course he wouldn't. That was why I'd used the word in the first place. "Tomorrow I'm going to talk to Lucy Perez and Candace Morgan again. Maybe something I've missed there will put me back on the track."

"Does that mean you'll need Dot and Lucy's guardian there again?"

He nodded. "And you will have a hard time believing this, but after tonight I'm going to ask you to go with Dot for this."

Fernandez was right; I did have a hard time believing that. "To what do I owe this sudden confidence?"

Ray shrugged. "It's been helpful to talk about this with somebody outside my usual contacts. No matter what I've said about you before, you're perceptive, Gracie Lee. If you just sit back and listen to all of this going on, you might hear something in a different way."

Wow. Ray's admission made me wish for a tape recorder, because I might not hear something like that from him again. I wanted to mark the moment for posterity. "Definitely, I'll go with Dot when you need her. Maybe this will clear Matt for you."

"And maybe it won't." Ray's eyes held sadness as he said that. It made me think of him as much more human and compassionate than I'd considered before. He didn't always like what his job made him do. I felt like reaching out and patting his hand or something, but then I came to my senses. This man had been close to arresting Ben less than forty-eight hours ago. Giving him sympathy felt like fraternizing with the enemy. Granted he changed that enemy status a little bit with this dinner and conversation, but still . . .

"For most of the people I know I'd say you should go home and pray on it, but we both know you're not a praying man. Yet."

He cocked his head back a bit and looked at me speculatively. "Does that 'yet' mean that you think I will be some day?"

"Hope springs eternal. And I've already learned that with God, nothing is impossible."

Ray shook his head. "Gracie Lee, if anybody, including God, can make a praying man out of me, I want to see it."

"Then we're both on the same page for a change, because I wouldn't mind seeing it, either." This felt like a good place to break off the dinner and conversation. He couldn't tell me much more about the case or Matt tonight, and I wasn't going to convince him of my views, either. And if we stopped here I might not say anything to get myself into trouble. "Ray, I had a great time having dinner with you."

"Surprisingly, I can say the same thing. When you're not sticking your nose where it doesn't belong you're a good listener."

"Thanks, I think." It sounded like the most back-handed compliment I'd gotten in a long time. "And definitely thanks for the dessert."

"My pleasure." I got up from the table and he followed. "Let me walk you out to your car. I'd hate to think I let you go out there alone in the dark. It goes against my better judgment."

"Why? Is it actually that dangerous in the strip malls of Ventura County?"

"No, but when I leave you alone too long, you find bodies and I've got all I can handle right now." His grin told me that Ray and I were back on our familiar footing before we'd ever left *Mi Familia* to go out into the crisp night air.

Wednesday morning while I helped Buck with the dog pen work I told him about Fernandez's plan to question Candace and Lucy again. I also told him that I could go with Dot this time if she wanted me to. "That might work real well," Buck said. "We're scheduled to do some therapy dog visits today, and if you went with Dot I could still manage Hondo and Dixie for their rounds at the hospital."

"Fine, then I'll go with her. While I think of it, how has Frankie Collins done helping you?" This was the first time I'd worked in the pens since Monday morning

156

now that Buck had started training Frankie.

"He prefers Frank, Jr. now. The kid is growing up too fast, I think, but most boys would in his situation. He's caught on quick to most of the work, but it's easy to see he's never done anything like manual labor before. And he's very interested in the investigation into his dad's death."

I shivered a little. "Sounds a bit grim."

Buck shrugged. "I think it goes with that growing up fast. He wants to make sure he's safe, and his mom and sisters are safe, and he figures that if the police arrest somebody for the murder, they can all rest easier."

It saddened me to think a boy of only thirteen had to think about things like that, and I told Buck that. "Don't think he's only interested in that, Gracie Lee. We also talked about who's going to be in the Super Bowl and what the so-called music was that was thumping out of the headphones he wore. He's still a kid."

That made me feel a little better as I went back to the apartment. By noon Dot called to tell me that we were on for three in Camarillo. "I'm not sure how much more Candace or Lucy could possibly tell that detective, but I don't see how asking more questions would hurt any, either," she said. "At first I worried that all this would upset Candace, but she seems calmer about everything the more she talks about Frank."

I offered to drive this time, and Dot agreed. The trip home would likely put us on the 101, a major freeway, at rush hour and I knew how she disliked that. "To make up for it I'll drive tomorrow night when we go to church to pack shoeboxes."

"Great. We'll be even then," I told her before we hung up. Then I dug around the apartment for my contribution to those shoeboxes because I'd totally forgotten until Dot mentioned it that the Christian Friends were slated to help pack personal care boxes for women and children at homeless shelters around the county. Different small groups in the church helped with the project before the holidays and we had agreed that this sounded like a great service project for Christian Friends. Somewhere I had a dozen washcloths bought at the warehouse store just for this purpose, along with a bag of shampoo and lotion samples that came in the mail.

By the time I'd found all of that and set it aside for Thursday night it was time to change clothes and get ready to drive Dot to Camarillo. There was little traffic going there and we pulled up in front of the group home just in time to see Fernandez get out of his car. "Good afternoon, Mrs. Morgan, Ms. Harris." So today we were back to formalities. That was fine with me, actually. I still wasn't sure what to make of the Ray Fernandez I'd encountered last night at the restaurant. "I thought we'd wait out here for Ms. Perez to join us."

We didn't wait long. In a few short minutes a relatively new compact buzzed down the street at a faster clip than I would have gone on a residential street, pulled a U-turn two houses down and stopped in back of Ray's unmarked car. A dark-haired woman of medium height, dressed in blue hospital scrubs, got out of the car and strode over to Ray. "This better be good because I can only stay about half an hour before I have to go back to the hospital." By the time she finished her sentence she was basically in Ray's face.

I expected fireworks, but Fernandez surprised me. "I'll try to make things as quick as possible, Ms. Perez. I can't promise I'll be done in half an hour but I'll do my best."

With that we all headed up the walk and Ray knocked on the door. Kirsten answered and ushered us all in.

"Hey, nice to see you again," she said to me. "And I really appreciate you coming, Estella. I don't feel all that comfortable standing in for you when this is a police matter."

Estella tossed her head, whipping around a long coffee-colored braid three fingers thick. "It's not like Lucy has done anything wrong. Besides, I don't think she could lie about anything to save her own life."

Maybe not, but saving Matt might be another story. Lucy and her sister settled on one end of the table in the dining room, while Dot and Candace sat on the other end. I pulled up a side chair and sat sort of behind them where I wasn't part of the group as much, and Ray made himself comfortable in a straight-back chair pulled up to the long side of the table.

"Okay, Candace, Lucy, I know I asked you plenty of questions when I came before but now I want to go over some of what we talked about again." He looked through his notes, turning pages for a moment. Then he turned his gaze to Candace. "You said that your cousin

159

Frank wasn't nice to you, and that he acted 'bad' with Lucy. Can you explain what you mean about the way he acted, Ms. Morgan?"

Candace sat quietly for a moment until Dot leaned in and said softly "Candace, he means you. You're Ms. Morgan."

"I know, Mom. I'm thinking." How much abstract thought on this level was Candace capable of? If the communication between Frank and Lucy had been nuanced with adult meanings, would she and Lucy have caught everything Frank meant? "Frank wasn't nice to anybody. He always tried to get free food from my restaurant and he got mad when I wouldn't do it. With Lucy, he tried to act like he was her boyfriend."

Lucy became visibly upset with that remark. "Frank is *not* my boyfriend. Nobody but Matt is *ever* going to be my boyfriend."

Her sister laid a hand on her arm. "It's okay, Lucy. Nobody's accusing you of anything. Candace is just telling the police officer how Frank wasn't nice to you."

"She's right. He wasn't nice to me. Besides, Frank is old and he's married. I don't want an old, married boyfriend."

If the subject weren't so serious I would have been tempted to laugh. Even Lucy knew that Frank was up to no good and called him on it.

Ray looked at Estella. "I'd like to ask Lucy if Collins made . . . uh . . . advances toward her."

"Then go ahead and ask her. She isn't deaf and she speaks for herself." If Estella was Lucy's advocate it

160

was a little hard to tell from her attitude. Maybe she was just trying to foster independence in her sister.

Ray seemed to be consulting his notes again. "Lucy, Matt has told me that he hit Frank because Frank wasn't nice to you. Did Frank ever try to do anything intimate with you?"

Lucy's face clouded. "Estella, you said I could speak for myself. But I don't understand exactly what he means."

Estella leaned in close to Lucy and spoke in a low voice. Her words were soft enough that no one else could hear all of them, but I could hear the occasional word, like "babies." After that, Lucy shook her head violently.

"Oh, no. He didn't do that. Besides, me and Candace, we're the same. We can't have any babies. Right, Estella?" She looked at her sister for confirmation, and Estella gave a small nod.

"Does that satisfy you, Detective Fernandez?" Estella crossed her arms over her chest and seemed to stare Ray down. It was the first time I had ever seen him look away from a confrontation first.

"On that issue it does, if you agree to what your sister says."

"Like I said before, Lucy doesn't know how to lie. She doesn't have the skills for deceit like the rest of us." Was that pride or sorrow in her sister's eyes when she talked about Lucy? I'd have to know Estella Perez much better to be able to tell.

"Okay, one more question. Did Matt tell you what

happened when he got into the fight with Frank, Lucy?"

"Matt said he hit Frank. And then Candace's mom took me to the funeral and she said Frank was dead and he was in that box and he couldn't bother me anymore."

"Did Candace's mom tell you that Frank wouldn't bother you? Are you sure that's the way it happened?" Ray's voice was gentle but firm and I knew what he was thinking.

Lucy looked down at the table in confusion. "No, wait. Candace's mom just told me Frank was dead. Matt told me Frank wouldn't bother me anymore. He said he took care of everything. I like the way Matt takes care of everything."

Silence hung over the table like a visible cloud. "Are we done here, Detective Fernandez?" Estella had an arm around her sister again.

"I believe we are, Ms. Perez." Ray closed his notebook and stood up.

"Does my sister need a lawyer? Will she have to testify in court?"

Ray shook his head. "No on both counts. Any competent defense attorney would eat her for lunch if she was on the stand in a trial. I wouldn't put either of you through that even if I thought it would help."

Dot and I looked at each other and I could tell we were thinking the same thing. The moment we got out of here we needed to call Lexy. Matt Seavers was going to need a good criminal lawyer, and fast.

Lucy watched Ray leave, but didn't get up from the

table. "Am I in trouble? Did I do something wrong? He looked mad."

Surprisingly her sister didn't move to comfort her right away, but stood up and looked like she was gathering her things together. "Lucy, you're okay. You're always okay. But I've got to go to work now." Estella gave her a brusque hug and headed to the door.

The difference in the way she dealt with her sister and the way Dot did with Candace felt like night and day. Dot went over to Lucy, who still sat looking confused. "You're not in trouble, Lucy. Telling the truth is always the best thing, even when it may cause somebody else a problem."

Dot sat down in the chair Estella had vacated. She faced Lucy and held her hands, and I could tell that she was going to try and explain to this young woman what her words might have brought about. But before she could, Candace came over beside her roommate. "Matt may be good at solving problems, Lucy, but I know somebody even better, right, Mom? It's Jesus. He can solve any problem."

"You're right, Candace. Lucy, do you want us to pray with you to ask Jesus to help ease any trouble Matt might be in right now?"

Lucy nodded, and before we left to call Lexy we gathered there in the dining room of Rose House to pray together. When we left Candace was comforting Lucy and both of them looked much calmer again.

"Prayer works in every situation," Dot murmured out on the front walkway. "I can't believe it took a reminder

163

from Candace for me to pray first and seek human aid second."

For once I didn't have anything to add to her thoughts, so I just kept praying silently that Jesus would look after all of us, including Estella at work and Ray Fernandez while he made a hard decision. They were the people who would probably be hurting most in this situation because it didn't look like either of them had much faith to lean on in a crisis.

Chapter Fourteen

God bless Lexy Adams for her quick thought and knowledge of the law. By the time we were all stuffing shoeboxes together at Conejo Community Chapel Thursday night she had lined up a good criminal defense attorney willing to take Matt's case for next to nothing. "There's always somebody willing to work pro bono if you look around a bit," she said as she went down the line dropping sample-sized bottles of shampoo into the personal care packages.

I followed behind her with washcloths rolled up into a cylinder. "So does your friend think Matt's going to need much of her services?"

"This time my attorney friend is a guy named Brian, and I haven't talked to him again since he met with Matt." Lexy went over to the table where the rest of the supplies sat stacked in plastic bags and picked up more shampoo. "But based on what you and Dot said about the interviews with Candace and Lucy, it wouldn't take much more for the sheriff's department to want to charge him."

"Exactly what would it take?" Dot stood next to us, dropping small bars of soap into each shoebox.

Lexy shifted the bag of shampoo bottles and ticked things off on her fingers. "Any real physical evidence linking Matt with the murder would be enough. Finding his fingerprints on the gun, or close to where they retrieved the gun. Or any admission of guilt he made to the police personally."

"They already have his fingerprints on the gun." I didn't know who else knew this. After I spoke I realized I might be getting myself in trouble with Fernandez again, but so be it. Lexy and her friend needed to know everything possible to defend Matt.

"Lovely. Does Matt have any explanation for how they got there?"

"He probably does and it more than likely related to the fistfight Matt and Frank got into. Ray told me the prints were on the barrel of the gun, not on the trigger or the butt or grip or whatever you call it on a pistol."

Lexy raised an eyebrow. "Hey . . . when did the detective become Ray?"

Oh, boy. Now I would be in trouble on two issues. "We bounce back and forth between formality and informality depending on whether he's mad at me or not. And we might have had dinner together at the same restaurant Tuesday night and talked a bit about the case."

"*Might* have had dinner together? Aren't you sure?"

Lexy wore a full grin now. Her teasing expression made her look even more like a high school cheerleader than usual.

"Okay, we had dinner together. But it wasn't a date or anything. He just came into the place where I was already having fish tacos, and neither of us felt like sitting alone."

"Gracie Lee, you don't have to explain to me. You're both over twenty-one and single, you know."

"That's true. But don't make more of this than there really is to it. Having a plate of fish tacos together does not make the basis for a relationship."

Lexy shrugged. "I've heard of relationships based on less. Of course I usually hear about that kind because one of my associates at the firm is dealing with a divorce. But getting back to the real subject at hand, which isn't good news. Matt's prints being on the gun aren't a good thing for him even if they're only on the barrel."

Dot had joined our little group. "You're right. And I'm worried about Matt anyway, because I don't know how he'll act if the police start questioning him in a serious way," she said. "I've seen him several times with Lucy and while he might be a little bit quicker than her, or Candace, he's always struck me as someone who would say something because he thought that was what somebody wanted to hear."

"That's the worst kind of person to have as a suspect to a crime." Lexy frowned. "There are more bogus confessions obtained because of people like that. Let's just hope your homicide detective recognizes Matt for what he is."

I shook my head. "He's not *my* homicide detective. In fact, I'd be willing to say Ray's not anybody's detective except his own. He'll follow procedure, but I don't think he'd try to get a false confession out of anybody."

"We can certainly pray that that's the case." Dot dropped the last individual pack of tissues into another shoebox. She looked down at the row of boxes, a thoughtful look on her face. "You know, Paula's the event chairperson for these boxes, and she says she needs at least a hundred more of them after we're done tonight. It's the kind of work that Lucy and Candace could do. Maybe I ought to see if they would like to be part of a work crew Saturday morning."

"That sounds like a good idea. Maybe they can bring some of their friends. And I'd certainly be happy to be part of the crew." Lexy smiled, and I could see the wheels turning in her head. I wondered who Lucy and Candace's "friends" would be on Saturday. I told Dot to count me in if she needed more people. With everyone who was likely to be involved, this was one group I wanted to see work together.

On Friday Dot called me to let me know about Saturday. "We're on for 10:00 a.m. filling more boxes. Candace, Lucy and I are going to grab a quick breakfast and go to the church from there. Do you want to go with us?"

"Not this time. I'll meet you at the chapel when it's

time to work on the kits. Before that I'll need to see that Ben gets something to eat, and I probably need to go grocery shopping this afternoon to make sure there's something I can fix for dinner tomorrow night."

Before the grocery store I made a quick stop at one of the "dollar store" places that abound here and picked up a few more washcloths and combs for the personal care boxes. I can't afford to do a lot of monetary giving right now, but I can definitely do something. Most of my church contribution is in time, like packing the boxes. Still, the thought of people without a roof overhead trying to live out of their cars or inside shelters haunts me and I want to spend money to help anybody in that situation.

There were a few cars in the lot when I got to the chapel the next morning. Nobody had a huge work crew packing boxes inside, judging from the amount of vehicles there.

I had been right in my supposition on Thursday night. The group around the table filling shoeboxes included not only Lexy, Dot, Candace and Lucy, but a young man who had to be Matt Seavers as well. Looking at him in the flesh, so to speak, I could see how somebody could confuse him and Ben, especially from the back. Matt was tall and rangy like Ben and like many guys in their teens and early twenties, favored hooded sweatshirts and baggy shorts. Today the shorts had been replaced by equally baggy jeans because it was cool and drizzly out again. Even I hadn't opted for sandals, wearing tennies for comfort.

"Hi, Gracie Lee. Come over here and meet Matt," Dot called when she saw me standing in the doorway with my bag of supplies. She did the introductions and I got a shy "hello" from Matt. He didn't meet my gaze for very long and it made me worry about how things might have gone at the sheriff's department. If he'd acted that way with Fernandez, the detective may have labeled him "shifty."

"Matt was just telling us about his experience yesterday at the sheriff's department," Lexy said while she dropped bars of soap into a row of shoeboxes. "He hasn't been charged with anything yet, although he was fingerprinted and questioned for a while."

"Yeah. They weren't real rough or anything. I was scared they were going to be," he said, still looking other places besides my face or anyone else's. Lucy hovered next to him, with the pair of them taking turns putting small bottles of shampoo into the boxes. They made quite a contrast, the tall young man with relatively plain features and the beautiful woman, even younger, much shorter and more rounded in her velour jogging suit.

"I invited Estella to come work with us this afternoon, but she had to be at the hospital," Dot said.

"That's okay with me." Matt gave a weak smile. "I don't think she likes me much."

Lucy patted his hand. "Sure she does. Estella is just cranky. She's that way with everybody."

"Everybody but you, Lucy." He leaned his head down to touch hers in a gesture of affection that was so sweet it made my throat tighten up. If this young man was a murderer, he was also an incredible actor, and I couldn't see that being the case.

An hour passed quickly as we made circuits of the table with different items for each shoebox. Working together we could do sixteen boxes at a time, all put next to each other on each side of the table. After a while you tended to get a little dizzy or stir-crazy or something, going around the circuit. Dot started singing a silly version of the hokey-pokey that had everybody giggling, even Matt. "I should have talked Buck into coming and doing this with us," she said, looking at Matt. "That way you wouldn't have been the only male member of this party."

Matt shrugged. "I don't mind. I work with guys all day, and this way I get to spend time with Lucy. This is cool."

"Yeah. We don't get to spend that much time together." Lucy moved even closer to him. "This is real nice."

"Do you two ever get to go out on dates?" Lexy asked.

Matt shook his head. "Not very often. I don't have a car or a license, so I have to count on somebody else for a ride. If I can get a ride to Lucy's place, we can walk someplace together, like the movie theater where she works."

"Yeah. I can get free tickets any night but Friday if I'm not working. I still have to pay for popcorn, but we don't eat much," Lucy added.

"So that's your social life?" Lexy's voice held a little sadness.

"Pretty much. Otherwise there's some kind of social event that ARC puts on once a month and that's about it."

I didn't have to ask Matt what ARC was. Hanging around Dot, I knew the letters stood for Association for Retarded Citizens, a term that wasn't used much anymore. Still, the agency kept its acronym just because the people who used their services were familiar with the term. Everything else they put out in the community talked about serving the developmentally disabled, which is the current "correct" term. Personally after meeting Candace, Lucy and Matt and a few of their friends, I had decided that "child of God" just like the rest of us was as appropriate as anything.

"How has your employer been about all of this?" Lexy was full of questions for Matt. I wondered if it was because of concern for him, or if these were things her friend Brian, the criminal lawyer, needed to know for something.

"Okay so far. If they arrest me I'm going to be in trouble with Leopold Plumbing. They don't like to have people with police records working for them."

Lexy frowned. "They can't fire you for that, Matt. Not unless they want a lawsuit on their hands."

He shrugged, looking down at the table. "They're smart. They'd find some other reason. I really hope it doesn't come up, because if I stay on there, I've got a chance at making journeyman soon. That would mean enough money that . . . well, it would mean good things."

Lucy smiled softly, looking at him. "Estella isn't here, Matt. And nobody will tell her. You can say it."

"Right," Candace piped up. "If you make more money, maybe you and Lucy could get married. She's doing real good in her independent living class."

Matt gave Candace a worried glance, then looked away. "Maybe you shouldn't say that, Candace. Maybe somebody would tell Estella anyway."

"I wouldn't," Lexy said firmly. "And I think everybody would agree that you can certainly talk about anything you want to. Now when it gets past the stage of talking and you start making plans, then it would be a good thing to talk to Estella, I think."

Lucy's sweet face clouded. "Estella will get mad. She always does. Then she'll say no. She doesn't think I should ever get married. Estella says I'll never be old enough to get married, old enough in my brain, anyway."

I didn't have any answer for that, so I stayed silent. Nobody else piped up right away either. For a few minutes we all just loaded different items into the shoeboxes instead.

After about twenty minutes more of making the rounds of the table, Linnette came into the room with a tray. "Okay, I think it's time for a break in here. The other group from one of the women's' prayer circles had refreshments set out. When they found out how large a group we had working in here, they insisted I

172

take a tray. Who wants cookies and hot cider?"

She didn't get many arguments. All work stopped and we sat at a table away from the shoeboxes, having a little social time together. It was only a little social time because before anyone had finished more than two cookies or half a cup of cider, someone else came into the room, putting a damper on our party.

"Matthew Seavers?" My heart sank as I heard Ray Fernandez use Matt's formal name that way. I knew what was likely to follow such formality.

Matt must have guessed, too, because he set down his cup, hugged Lucy while whispering something in her ear, and stood up. "Yes, sir?"

"You are under arrest for suspicion of murder in the death of Frank Collins." Fernandez continued on with the full words of a Miranda warning while putting a set of handcuffs on Matt. Lexy was alternately spluttering and dialing something into her cell phone before Ray got half of the words out.

"I don't think it's right to do that in a church, Mom," Candace said, her lower lip trembling.

"I'm not sure it's right to do anywhere, but that remains to be seen," her mother answered.

"Brian Naylor will be at the sheriff's station before you even finish booking his client." Lexy's face was flushed and her hands shook as she closed up her cell phone.

"I wouldn't have it any other way, Ms. Adams." The detective looked saddened and grim as he glanced my way, leading the now-handcuffed Matt toward the door.

Ray's golden brown eyes seemed to be asking for forgiveness. If I had felt like speaking to him, which I didn't, I would have told him that I wasn't in the mood for forgiveness right now.

Instead of saying anything to him while he and Matt left, I concentrated on Lucy instead. She stood near where Matt had left her, tears running down her smooth cheeks. "I knew it. I got him in trouble. They're taking Matt to jail." The last word stretched out to several syllables as she sobbed while trying to speak.

"Lexy's friend will make sure he doesn't stay in jail any longer than he has to." It was small comfort but the best I could give from a human perspective. "Why don't we all pray for Matt again like we did the other day?"

"Okay. Can we go to the big room, the house room?"

"Okay, if you want to," I told her. "Let's tell Candace's mom where you want to go."

I repeated Lucy's words, hoping that Dot would enlighten me as to exactly where we were going. Dot looked puzzled for a minute, then her face cleared. "You mean the sanctuary, Lucy? Where they had Frank's funeral, right?"

Lucy nodded. "Somebody said that's God's house. I thought maybe He'd hear us better this time if we went to His house."

Dot put an arm around Lucy and handed her a tissue to wipe her face. "Lucy, God hears us wherever we pray, because God is with us wherever we are. But if you feel better talking to Him in the sanctuary, then that's where we'll go."

We sat in the front row of the upholstered chairs that the Chapel uses instead of pews, all of us linked and holding hands in a line. It was far more difficult for me to add Ray to my prayers this time. I knew he was only doing his job, but it still bothered me that he'd take Matt away like that in front of Lucy and the rest of us in a church building.

"Will you help me take the girls back to Rose House? I think they need to be in familiar surroundings," Dot said as we left the sanctuary.

"Sure. Let me grab my purse from the classroom and I'll be ready to go." We could always swing by later and get my car.

Kirsten looked troubled when we told her why Candace and Lucy were back earlier than planned, and why Lucy especially seemed so upset. "I ought to call her sister right away and let her know about this. But that will cause as many problems as it solves." She sighed, watching the roommates head toward their bedroom. "I think Estella's ready to pull Lucy out of Rose House because of all the commotion. Although what she'd do with her while she works all those shifts at the hospital is beyond me."

"Maybe it won't come to that. Maybe this will all settle down soon and the police will figure out they've made a mistake in arresting Matt." Dot sounded hopeful while she said that, but I could see that the hope in her voice didn't carry over to her eyes.

Sunday after church I think we all felt pretty glum. Dot caught up with me after the service while I waited for Ben. My suspicions of the week before had proved correct; there was a cute girl in the praise band that he just had to talk with after the service. I tried to contain my curiosity and not speculate which of the three young ladies close to his age was the one. While he chatted, I stood out in the narthex where I wouldn't embarrass him.

"Lexy's friend wasn't able to get Matt out of jail right away. But Lexy says we can plan strategy over dinner tonight." I'd almost forgotten that we had the Christian Friends potluck.

"See you at six," I told her and Dot hurried on. I looked at my watch, wondering how much longer Ben would spend in the sanctuary. Just about then he appeared with a funny grin on his face.

"Sorry. I didn't mean to leave you stranded out here, Mom. If Kylie had a car, I'd just tell you to go on without me, but she caught a ride with one of her friends, so I can't very well tag along. Could you take me home so I could drive back up here and offer her a ride after the next service?"

"Would Kylie be the mystery woman you went to the movies with?" Things were beginning to add up. Ben nodded, but didn't say much more, leaving me to do the talking. "Sure, I can take you home. Do you want to grab a quick bite of early lunch someplace while we're out?"

"Yeah. Not much, because I want to offer to take her out for a late lunch or coffee at least if she can go, but I'm starving. How about In-N-Out?"

It sounded good to me, so we headed to the hamburger stand that is the epitome of Southern California for me. How anybody can eat a normal fast-food hamburger after going to In-N-Out is beyond me. Everything's fresh, the staff is made up of unfailingly cheerful teens and they have John 3:16 printed on their drink cups. What could possibly be better?

Even on Sunday it didn't take us that long to make a quick burger and fries run and get Ben back home to pick up his car. While he dashed back to church, I stayed at the apartment for a little while, putting together my dish for the potluck. I wondered if it really mattered what anybody fixed, or if we'd all be so busy talking about Matt that the food would go by the wayside. Thinking about other Christian Friends gatherings, I decided to still put just as much effort into my chicken casserole. This bunch always needed sustenance while we thought and planned. We seemed to do our best work over coffee and dessert.

Chapter Fifteen

The Christian Friends meeting that night was supposed to be our Christmas potluck. We all still brought food, but the meeting was much more somber than any Christmas party I'd ever been to before. Mostly the meeting turned into a working dinner and planning session on how to get Matt out of jail as quickly as possible. It took a while to come up with any concrete, realistic ideas.

First Lexy had to explain to the rest of us why Matt got charged with suspicion of murder in the first place. According to her, the fact that it was second-degree murder should make us all relieved. I wasn't so sure. "It really all boils down to one handprint," she said over Dot's tempting broccoli salad. "Before they found that, nothing else added up to enough to charge him."

"So why does one print make the difference?" Dot, of course, was enjoying my chicken casserole—Mom's recipe—and Heather's chili-cheese dip far more than her own salad. Nobody ever seems to like their own stuff best at a potluck dinner, no matter how tasty it is.

"Before the hand print, the three key steps for charging somebody with murder were there, but they were pretty weak." We must have all looked confused then, because Lexy went on. "Police look for means, motive and opportunity. The means were there, but due to the lack of prints where it matters, *anybody* could have shot Frank Collins with his own gun. Matt had motive, but it was not the world's strongest. Granted, men have murdered each other before for hitting on a girlfriend, but Matt doesn't seem like that type of guy."

"Opportunity was there," Dot supplied, as realization dawned on her. "Buck and I proved Matt had the opportunity when we told the detective we'd seen Matt talking to Frank in the driveway."

"Right." Lexy waved a fork to make her point. Fortunately it was a clean fork. "But you saw Matt talking to Frank when both were upright and in seemingly good shape. And you didn't see a real fight, correct?"

"No pushing, shoving or hitting," Dot agreed. "And since the windows were rolled up in the van, we couldn't tell whether they yelled at each other or not."

"So at that point the police had a lot of things that could tie Matt to the murder, but probably none any stronger than they might have on Darnell or any of several other guys working on the remodeling project. Then they found the handprint inside the portable toilet."

"But that could have been there for weeks. You can't date a fingerprint or handprint, can you?" That bothered me the most. Probably a dozen of the guys' prints could show up inside that facility. As far as that went, they most likely found my prints in there, too. But most of the prints including mine had been made while using the facility for the intended use, not stowing a murder victim.

"No, you can't date prints, not the way you're talking about. It would have been a lot stronger evidence if the handprint had smeared blood in or under it, of course. Even without that kind of evidence, though, a good prosecutor will use that print to argue that Matt could have put it there while disposing of the body."

"But it's not like they have a witness to anything like that, right?" Heather hadn't added much to the conversation so far, using most of her time instead to feed Corinna lovely stuff out of jars and eat a few bites from the buffet herself once the baby slept. Since I remembered having a little one on the verge of walking and talking, with all that boundless energy, I couldn't fault her a bit for taking care of herself. Ten-month-old babies weren't known for their patience, so their parents had to be resourceful.

When you added to that the fact that Heather was doing all the parenting alone, it was a double burden. Right now Corinna looked like a doll, sleeping in her stroller while wearing an adorable red velvet Christmas dress. Half an hour from now the baby would probably look more like a hurricane, awake and shrieking for attention.

For the present, she slept on, letting her mother and the rest of us talk about Matt's problems. "You're right, Heather, there are no witnesses to the murder. If somebody had seen anything while it went on, we wouldn't need to have this conversation. We'd know for certain whether Matt had been involved in this whole mess." Lexy drew a design in the ranch dip on her plate with a carrot stick. It was easy to see how she stayed so skinny. Anyone who would rather play with their food than eat it could fit in size four jeans like she undoubtedly did.

"Witnesses or not, I still don't think Matt's capable of killing anybody, even Frank Collins." Dot looked like the protective mother hen she usually was, only now she had more than one chick to look after.

"I agree with Dot. I've only met the young man once, but he just doesn't strike me as the kind of person who could kill someone, even in anger." Of course I could be wrong. But I really hoped I wasn't because Matt Seavers seemed like a pleasant person. Of course that's what the neighbors always tell the newspaper reporters

180

when they're talking about serial killers, isn't it?

"Fortunately the presiding judge agrees with you." Lexy went on to actually eat her carrot stick. When she finished with it, she went on. "He's apparently open to Brian making a motion to get Matt released on his own recognizance, or maybe into Brian's custody. Without a car or a license, and having a steady job he's likely to keep, the young man isn't a flight risk. Coupled with the fact that he has no criminal record, it should be relatively easy to get him out of jail."

"Couldn't we just bail him out?" Heather rocked the stroller while she talked. Lexy shook her head.

"Nope. Nobody Matt knows has the kind of money he'd need to get out. The Ventura County bail schedule starts murder bail bonds at five hundred thousand."

Heather gulped. "Half a million dollars? That's incredible. Nobody could pay that, could they?"

"You're right. Even what somebody would have to give a bail bondsman, which would be fifty thousand dollars, is more than anybody I know would risk at this point."

"More than I'd be willing to spend on bailing somebody out of jail who probably belongs there in the first place." Paula's lip curled in contempt. Too bad she held that opinion, because the real estate agent might have been the one Christian Friend who would have connections to someone with enough money to bail Matt out.

Dot looked at Paula in consternation. "Now how can you say that? I don't think you've ever met Matt."

Paula's chin rose. "Actually, I have. Leopold

181

Plumbing redid the wet bar in our game room. They did a decent job but charged us double what our old contractor did. When I complained about it, Matt Seavers had the nerve to tell me that none of the other firm's work would pass code."

Given the strict nature of Ventura County's codes on remodeling, I imagined Matt had been right. That wouldn't have made it any easier for Paula to hear, especially coming from somebody as young-looking and tentative as Matt. In her line of work she expected to be right most of the time, and not crossed.

Lexy appeared to be trying to be diplomatic. "I'm sorry to hear you don't think much of Matt, but I don't see what his lack of tact has to do with his likelihood of being a murderer."

Paula sniffed. "Anybody who could be that rude to a paying customer certainly doesn't have any respect for others."

Dot shook her head and rolled her eyes but stayed silent. Paula couldn't see the gesture from where she sat, but I could. Still, I didn't even think of laughing because I'd already promised myself that I would be as kind to Paula as possible. Her prickly nature hid a wounded heart just like any of ours. It was a pity she didn't like Matt, though.

"Does Brian need money for expenses? I know he's doing this pro bono, but there have to be things involved that cost money," Dot said.

Lexy shrugged. "There are things, but Matt's family doesn't have any money. Brian talked to his father, for all the good it did. Matt basically supports him, not the other way around. Even if the man had any extra money, Brian said he expected it would go for alcohol, not helping his son. Brian's just a good-hearted Christian guy who will eat the costs."

"That's too bad. We'll just have to work on it ourselves," Dot said, getting that stubborn look I'd seen more than once on my friend. "I imagine I can talk Buck out of the three hundred dollars we got for that last puppy of Sophia's. If he argues I'll tell him it will be instead of the diamond earrings I asked for this Christmas."

"Buck is getting you diamond earrings?" Linnette looked surprised.

Dot grinned. "No, but I always ask for them. I always get something far more practical, like a new blender but that doesn't keep me from putting them at the top of the Christmas list every year as a joke. Whether the package contains a blender or diamond earrings doesn't matter to either of us. And this year I'm happy for it to go toward help for Matt."

"I could probably come up with fifty dollars," Heather said softly. Her new teaching job at the closest community college covered the bills for her and Corinna, but didn't leave a lot afterward. Like me, she found herself challenged by losing her savings to Dennis Peete over year ago.

Paula's shoulders slumped. "I guess you could put me in for a hundred. Maybe Matt Seavers was just doing his job when we argued." It was easy to see she hated to be bested by someone of such limited means.

"Put me down for fifty," I told Lexy. It would be a stretch, but that inner voice that urged me to do things I didn't think possible was nudging me. I'd learned not to ignore that voice.

"Okay, that's enough to cover any out-of-pocket costs for Brian just over dinner. I wonder what I can get out of Steve if I make puppy eyes at him." Lexy had a grin to match Dot's. "And I haven't even talked to Linnette yet, or Pastor George about the church's emergency fund. We're making progress."

The meeting got a lot less somber from then on, especially when Linnette brought out a tray of cookies. There's nothing like chocolate, sugar and hope to lift the mood of a group of women.

I felt pretty chipper by the time I drove home after the meeting. We hadn't exactly solved all the world's problems, or even all of Matt's problems, but at least things looked better. When I pulled into the driveway Ben's car was there and through the window I could see the Christmas tree lights on.

When I opened the door I heard the familiar sounds of video games on the TV and saw my son sprawled out on the floor. The only surprise was that there was a young lady sitting close to him, also holding a controller and laughing while she apparently beat him at a game.

"See, I told you I could, and you didn't believe me," she crowed. The room got its light from the tree and the

TV screen, so I couldn't tell right away who this girl was. I had the suspicion, however, that this might be the mysterious Kylie. I flipped on the light switch next to the door, knowing it would probably earn me a howl from Ben. That was tough, because while I appreciated the art of playing video games in the dark, I didn't want him in the living room with a girl in the dark, even playing video games.

"Whoa. Hi, Mom." Ben looked up from his screen just long enough to say hello, then went back to the game. In less than a minute the screen was flashing with things like "game over" and "winner, player 2" that had Kylie laughing again and Ben putting down his game controller in disgust.

"Now that we're to a good stopping place, let me introduce you." Ben got his long legs untangled and stood up, putting out a hand to his friend to hoist her off the floor as well. She had a lot less trouble getting up, being compact to his gangliness. "Mom, this is Kylie. Kylie, this is my mom, Gracie Lee Harris. Kylie goes to school with me, Mom, and she's in the praise band at your church."

"Hi. Nice to meet you," the young lady said, bouncing up for the typical hug-and-air-kiss female California greeting. Her black hair was glossy and a wonderful sweet floral scent wafted around her.

"Nice to meet you, too. Ben's been talking about you some and I wondered how long it would be until I met you." Now that I had a chance to look at the mystery lady close up, I saw that I was going to have to mentally change the way I spelled her name. Instead of the Irish or Midwest American lass I'd expected with a name like Kylie, this girl was Asian. She was also pretty enough that I had to wonder what she saw in my scruffy-looking son with that awful goatee, but then it was grown to appeal to her, not me.

"Oh, so you've been talking about me?" she asked, looking up at him and arching one delicate eyebrow. I was quite thankful to see that said eyebrow had no rings or other jewelry pushed through it. In fact, what I could see of her didn't sport any unusual holes or piercings at all. Even her earrings were small and her speech was too crisp for a tongue stud.

Ben shrugged. "Not that much. I said we were going to the movies last week. And I might have said something about the praise band being good at the chapel." His smile looked softer when he talked to her. I hadn't ever seen Ben before with a girl he appeared to care much about. This was interesting.

"So, since you play in the praise band, does this mean you live here in town?" I had to keep making some conversation and that felt like a safe subject.

"My parents live in Newbury Park," she said, naming another suburb between Thousand Oaks and Camarillo.

"She's a scholarship student like me, so she lives in the dorm when school's in session. That's how we got to know each other, going to advising meetings together."

"Yeah, they were spectacularly boring, but at least they had benefits," Kylie said, grinning. How did she spell her name? It was a goofy detail that would aggravate me until I asked.

Instead of launching a question like that, which would have Ben doing an eye roll in front of her, I sat in the armchair while they took the couch and I cast about for another subject. I found one easily enough when they both picked up plastic drinking cups with huge straws poking through a taut sheet of plastic wrap. The contents of each cup had unidentifiable objects in the bottom of the cup, surrounded by pale liquid. Ben's was green; Kylie's was sort of a peachy orange.

"What on earth do you have there?" It was the strangest looking drink I'd ever seen, and I hoped it wasn't anything that would cause a family argument.

"Boba," they said in tandem, giving me that universal look that said I was hopelessly behind the times.

"Go on. Explain more. I have no idea what boba is, or are," I admitted, sealing my fate as a clueless parent.

"It's kind of like an ice-blended coffee, only not," Ben started. I felt like this was going to be a long, confusing explanation.

"Why don't you give her a sip of yours," Kylie suggested. "It's easier to explain once you've tasted it."

I wasn't all that sure I wanted to, but Ben was already proffering his cup. It had the weight and feel of an iced coffee, but there was something knocking against the side of the cup.

"Some places call it bubble tea," the girl said while I looked at the cup. My look must have been tentative because she kept on talking. "Ben's is green tea and mine is mango. They're really good." She had that tone I could remember trying with a toddler facing a spoonful of cauliflower.

I was in too deep to pull back now, so I took a sip on the huge straw. The sweet, icy liquid had a milky green tea flavor, but what really threw me was the marble-sized ball of something that bounced in my mouth with the liquid. I must have really looked surprised, because Ben laughed softly.

"You found one of the tapioca pearls. That's the stuff on the bottom, the black balls. I think they're fun."

"Hmm." I rolled the tapioca thing around, trying to figure out how I'd describe the texture. It was some-where between rubber and a ripe berry, and truly a unique experience. I thanked Ben, handed back his drink, and promised myself that this would be a unique experience for sure, because one taste of boba was enough for me.

Chapter Sixteen

Dot laughed the next morning while I described boba tea to her. "You're braver than I am. Candace and some of her friends enjoy that stuff, too, but I'm not trying it. My mother used to say tapioca looked like fish eyes, and that big black stuff looks even more like fish eyes than the little pearls you make pudding out of. No, thank you."

I admitted to her that it was probably a one-time experience for me. "I don't have enough desire for Ben to think I'm hip and trendy to try it again. It gave me the oddest combination of brain freeze and weird mouth feel that I've ever had. Maybe I did it just to impress his girlfriend."

"Oh? He brought home a girl?"

"Yes, one from school. She plays in the praise band at church, too. I thought he'd been awfully happy to go to services with me lately."

"I wouldn't recognize her from that. Buck says all praise songs sound alike to him, so I humor him and go to the traditional service with him."

I would beg to differ with him on that point, but it's the same thing my mom says. Maybe it just takes an open mind and younger ears to enjoy a praise band. There were always some people more my mom's age or Dot's at the contemporary service, but they weren't the majority.

"Is she a freshman like Ben?"

"I don't know. We didn't talk that long. Once I'd been introduced Ben decided it was time to take Cai Li home before I asked her too many questions. I don't know why he was so anxious to go. We'd only gotten through the basics, like whether her parents had grown up here or abroad and how many brothers and sisters she had."

I couldn't help grinning while I said all of that. For Ben it was probably way too much information for me to know how Cai Li spelled her name, that her parents came from Vietnam in the early 70s and that she had what she described as "two bratty little brothers" at home. And here I had just been getting started. She and I had been warming up to each other, but Ben got more antsy with each question and answer, until he finally almost pulled her out the door, insisting that he needed to get her home early for a change. I had to think he didn't want his brand-new girlfriend and his mother bonding just yet.

I could understand his argument if I really thought about it from his young, male point of view. But thanks to events he didn't even know much about, this was the only way I was ever going to experience anything close to having a daughter. My face must have shown some of what I was thinking, because Dot put a hand on my arm.

"Okay, where are you inside there? Do you want company?"

"I don't know. Just thinking about things that happened a long time ago. Sometimes I get a little jealous of all of you with daughters."

Dot was quiet for a while, looking at me with a gentle, knowing look. "You had one once, didn't you?" Dot asked softly.

"Yes, I did." I hadn't told anybody about this in years. "For six days. She was born prematurely, eighteen months after Ben. I was still very young, just past twenty-one, and when Emily died it was the beginning of the end for my marriage."

"Losing a child is one of those events that either strengthens a couple tremendously or pulls them apart." I felt thankful for them that Dot and Buck's troubles

190

apparently strengthened their relationship.

"Just losing her wasn't the thing that pulled us apart. It was the way that Hal and his mother took over while I spent all my time in the neonatal intensive care unit with our daughter that week. My parents were taking care of Ben, so I could be there. I couldn't do much for her, couldn't even hold her most of the time. She was so tiny and so frail. I wanted to name her Joanna Louise for two of our grandmothers."

"But you just called her Emily, so I have to assume that didn't happen."

I was crying now, but it felt good, and I could talk through the tears. "Right. After four days straight the nurses insisted that I go home, shower and sleep in my own bed. When I came back into the nursery the next morning, instead of the incubator saying "baby girl Harris" like it had before, it said Emily Jo Harris. I felt stunned.

"Hal's mother insisted that the baby had to be named and baptized before she died, and she was adamant that it happen *right then*. Hal didn't argue with her and somehow figured that I wouldn't, either. By the time I got back everything was done."

"Did the name mean something to Hal's mother?" Why did Dot always have to be so perceptive? Even my mother hadn't asked that question right away.

"Hal had an older sister who only lived two weeks. Her name was Emily. I was totally horrified that they would name our daughter, who was fighting so hard to live, for a little girl who had died. When Emily got a staph infection the next night, I never left her side again, but the damage had already been done to our marriage."

Dot handed me a tissue from somewhere and kept patting my arm. "You know, some day you ought to talk about this with the rest of the Christian Friends. They're very good listeners."

"I know. And most of the time I'm okay with this now. But thinking about Ben's girlfriend, and how I just *had* to talk to her last night made me wonder if I was trying to replace Emily just a little."

"Maybe so. I know I tend to latch on to bright, independent young women to give me a little bit of what I know I won't quite have with Candace, but I don't feel guilty about it anymore. I have a wonderful relationship with my daughter, and I figure God sends me other people, like you, Gracie Lee, to give me the things I miss."

I felt touched to think that Dot had adopted me even a little. Family is a funny concept sometimes. It often has as much to do with who we love and how we relate to people as it does with blood. The wise old pastor at Granny Jo's church back in Cape Girardeau used to say that folks said blood is thicker than water, but he believed that the baptismal water that made us all part of the family of God was thicker than any blood. "Thanks, Dot. I can always use another mom." Hugging her there in her kitchen made me wonder where Matt and Lucy's broader family came from, and how we needed to fit into that family to keep Matt from being held and even perhaps tried for a murder he didn't commit.

I'd barely gotten home from Dot's when she called me on the phone with unbelievable news. "Ed Leopold and at least one of his crew members want to come over and look at the bathroom." I could hardly believe our good fortune. Given that it was less than a week until Christmas, I'd figured that nothing else would happen until the New Year started, or perhaps even sometime around Groundhog Day. But by ten Mr. Leopold and his son Bob stood in the bathroom measuring, checking pipe joints and writing down whole bunches of things that didn't really make sense to me, but certainly did to them.

They turned down my offer of coffee and kept working in the bathroom for a while. Either Ben was so sound asleep that they weren't bothering him or he'd prudently decided not to put in an appearance in his pajamas. I retreated to the living room to glance at the newspaper and have a cup of the coffee I'd made. In twenty minutes or so, the Leopolds came out of the bathroom. Surprisingly enough they both had smiles on their faces.

"This isn't near as bad as I thought it would be," Ed told me, looking down at his legal pad full of notes. "Once I talk to Mrs. Morgan again and figure out just what she's paid on the missing fixtures, and who got the money, we can be good to go. I figure Wednesday or Thursday we could put in the second commode and do most of the finishing in that section. The plumbing and the bathtub will take a little longer, what with the tile that needs to go in, but definitely it'll be done before New Year's Eve."

"Wow. I know Dot will agree with me when I say that's a dandy present." I couldn't help asking what was on my mind. "How did we get so lucky, anyway? I figured that you all would be so slammed with other work that we'd be lucky to see you before spring."

Bob laughed. "You don't know my dad very well, then. He always schedules a lot of open time after Thanksgiving so that if any of our jobs get hung up before then, we can at least get them done before Christmas."

"And this year we stayed on schedule with everything but this one, honestly." Ed's smile went all the way to his eyes. "Besides, my wife would skin me alive if I wasn't ready to go up to the cabin at Lake Arrowhead by Christmas Eve. We've done it since this guy was in diapers and *my* parents owned the cabin."

It sounded like a great family getaway and I told him so. For a moment it made me sad that I wouldn't be having a big family Christmas this year myself. Ben would leave the end of the week to go see Hal, and my mom isn't the kind to surprise me by flying out. Just not her style. Hopefully Dot and Buck, or Linnette at least, would have room for me at one house or the other for the holidays. Spending them totally alone sounded awful.

Father and son made a few more notations and said

goodbye so they could go over and talk to Dot. Once they left I heard doors shutting in the bathroom and the shower turn on. Ben was up for another morning before eleven without prodding. Maybe having a girlfriend wasn't such a bad thing for him after all. I couldn't assume he was rising this early just to see me, but I'll cheerfully reap the benefits of him wanting to go out with Cai Li.

We had a cheerful conversation while he ate a bowl of cereal. At least my end was cheerful. His started by taking me to task. "Did you have to ask so many questions?"

"Sure. Why should meeting her be any different than meeting your other friends through the years? Face it— I knew more about Ted after having been in the suite ten minutes than you guys had found out in a week."

"Yeah, but was any of it important stuff?"

"It was to me. How's his break going, anyway?"

Ben really looked at me then like I'd sprouted a second head. "How would I know? He went back home to Wherevers-ville in Minnesota and I'll see him when we both get back to school." His disbelief that I'd actually expect him to talk to or e-mail his roommate was more than evident. I decided it wasn't a good time to point out that I still exchanged Christmas cards with my freshman-year roommate. Just the difference between the sexes, I guess.

It was time to start another subject. "So, what are your plans for the day?"

"We'll probably hit a couple thrift stores, have lunch

and maybe go for boba again." His grin was wicked. "Want us to bring you back one? Tapioca Express over in Simi Valley makes a blue raspberry milk tea one that is a blue I can't even describe."

I tried to suppress a shudder. "Thanks, but I'll pass. Feel free to bring your friend back anyway. And this time I'll try to keep my questions to a minimum."

"As if that's possible, Mom." At least he was smiling when he said it.

Ben soon went off to visit thrift stores or whatever it was that the two of them decided to do, and while he was gone I wrapped his Christmas presents. There wasn't a huge pile when I was done, but we'd never gone crazy with Christmas gifts anyway. Hal's parents always went so far overboard that I learned early on not to compete. True, Grandpa Roger and his current wife tended toward gift certificates to places like Abercrombie & Fitch that Ben wouldn't be caught dead shopping at. And Grandma Lillian, while she took a little more care in picking things out, still usually missed the mark.

I knew that the one video game—not the kind where any people blew up, thank you very much—and the DVD of a movie that he'd watched with Dave at least twice a week in seventh grade would go over well. The other things I wrapped were silly fun stuff like athletic socks with the Pacific Oaks panther mascot logo and a package of fine-point black pens in hopes that he wouldn't run off in January with all of mine in the apartment.

I thought about calling my mom while I wrapped gifts but knew she'd only cluck at me. Her gifts for the two of us had been shipped the day after Thanksgiving and had probably been wrapped somewhere around Halloween. I was just happy that I'd gotten her present, a spiffy "Pac Oaks Mom" sweatshirt and matching coffee mug, before the bookstore closed once finals were over. Only my proximity to the store while working at the Coffee Corner made me that efficient—that and Linnette nagging me more than once in the last month of school.

Even the little bit of wrapping I did kept me busy for a couple hours in the afternoon. When I got up off the floor and stretched—a process that takes longer and feels worse every year—the clock proclaimed it to be 3:00 p.m. already. Walking off the stiffness in my knees, I went to the large front window and could see Buck out by the dog pens talking to a dark-haired kid. It looked like I would finally have a chance to meet Frankie Collins.

It was one of those contrary days where the sun shone brightly but a little breeze kicked up now and then, making it feel cooler than the 70 degrees the porch thermometer registered. The Capri-length jeans and T-shirt that felt just fine inside made me shiver a little when that bit of wind caught me going down the outside stairs. Still, I didn't want to go back up and get a jacket and blow my Midwestern warm-blooded image. Besides, Frankie, like most kids his age, wore shorts with his impossibly large tennies and a long-sleeved T-shirt advertising a rock band in all its rude glory. He'd already think I was an old lady anyway, but I figured why confirm his beliefs.

Once I stood close to him he looked like exactly what he was, a slightly pudgy kid nowhere near needing to shave yet. I tried to remember where Dot said he was in school. Eighth grade stuck in my mind. That alone would explain why he hadn't looked up once from his dog pen cleaning, even if I couldn't see the headphones and portable CD player he wore. His head bobbed to the music as he halfheartedly worked with a hose.

"I'll introduce you when I can make eye contact." Buck's voice behind me nearly put me airborne. I'd always startled easily, much to Ben's delight. Now Buck put a large hand on my shoulder. "Sorry about that. Didn't mean to get you that stirred up."

"Not a problem. Anybody talking behind me does it. So how's he doing so far?"

I turned to look at Buck and could see him worrying the corner of his silver mustache with his tongue a little. "Well, about as good as I've found any kid his age to work out. He's prompt most of the time anyway."

Buck almost always found a good word to say about somebody, even when he said it in his gruff way. While punctuality was important to him, the fact that noting it was the best thing he could say about Frankie told me a lot about his quality of work. Still, the kid needed the money, so I knew Buck would be patient with him for quite a while.

"Ah, there he is," Buck said, and I turned around to

see Frankie come out of the pen he had finished with and slip off the headphones. "Frank, I want to introduce you to Gracie Lee. If Mrs. Morgan and I have to go any-where, Gracie Lee will be working with you. I probably should say *Mrs. Harris* will be the one telling you what to do. Gracie Lee, this is Frank Collins, Jr."

"Hey. Good to meet you, Frank." I put out my hand, but then realized he probably wouldn't shake it. Between being a young teen at an awkward phase and the tools he had to balance, it wouldn't work. When it became evident quickly that I was right, I put down my hand so as not to fluster him.

"Hi," he said more to the ground than my face. In an adult I could have taken offense at that; from a boy his age it was normal behavior. After a bit of a shuffle he looked up at Buck. "What else you got for me to do?"

"Have you ever brushed and groomed a dog before? Sophie could sure use it."

"Nuh-uh. Is it hard to do? I don't want to hurt her or anything."

"I wouldn't let you. Why don't I get the dog and Mrs. Harris will show you the tools and how to use them."

"Okay." Frankie put the hose and other equipment down without a lot of grace. I went over to and turned off the water without saying anything. Maybe if I mod-eled good behavior he'd catch on eventually. Or maybe I'd just have to be blunt and tell him what to do.

I went over to the supply cabinet next to the dog runs where Buck kept grooming equipment. Opening a drawer, I got out the brush and flea comb we'd use on

Sophie. I explained how to use them, and then held them out to Frankie. "Do you want to try it first, or watch me a little before you try it?"

He had a speculative look, eyes narrowed, that made me see a bit of his father in him. I could almost feel him debating which was worse; possibly making a fool of himself or taking instruction from a woman. Finally he gave a one-shouldered shrug. "I'll watch. Just for a little while."

Buck was leading sweet, docile Sophie toward us by then. She never complained about being groomed, so she was the best choice for this exercise. She and Dixie were Lab mix with something much furrier thrown in, like Shepherd or collie. "This is Sophie." Buck stopped and patted the wide grooming bench and she jumped up on it looking happy. He dropped the leash. "You don't have to leash her to anything while you groom her. Some of the other dogs you do, but you wouldn't want to start with them anyway. I'll leave you two to your work."

Without a lot of fanfare I started brushing the dog in long, easy strokes from her neck to hips. "She grows a heavier winter undercoat and that's what sheds if we don't brush her pretty often. It doesn't usually tangle, but don't jerk the brush or she'll grumble at you."

Frankie nodded, watching silently. After a few more strokes I stood back a step and handed him the brush. He was a little tentative at first, which was better than being too rough with her. At first he worked quietly. It was only after he had finished almost a whole side of

Sophie's dark body that he spoke. "I still get paid for this even if you're showing me how, right?" He sounded suspicious.

"Sure. You can't know how to do everything right away. Learning is part of the job."

"Good. I've got plans for the money already."

"Cool. Plans are good . . . you have a new CD in mind?" I asked, pointing down at his player.

He gave me a look more scornful than Ben would ever have dared. "Get real. I want to make sure the cops keep the lowlife who killed my dad locked up. Or maybe I can do something about it if they screw up and let him go."

I felt stunned into silence. His voice was so cold and calculating that for a moment I forgot this was only a thirteen-year-old next to me. He had a man's anger without a man's maturity. It was a dangerous combination I knew I needed to tell Ray Fernandez about, and soon.

Chapter Seventeen

Honestly, I expected Ray to be far more appreciative of my information. I only got voice mail that evening when I tried to reach him, so I left a bare-bones message. There are some things you just don't want to say over a phone, and discussing the possible murderous tendencies of a young teen was one of those things for me. By eight Tuesday morning my phone rang. "Is this worth my coming over there this early?" It wasn't the most pleasant greeting I'd ever gotten from him, but it wasn't the worst, either.

"I think it is. Should I put on coffee?"

"I'll grab some on the way. Should I bring you anything?"

"No, I'm okay with what I've got here," I told him and he hung up quickly. I made a face at the phone when I put it back in its cradle and went to the kitchen to make a fresh pot of coffee anyway. I was worth it even if he disdained my coffee.

No sooner had I started filling the coffeemaker carafe with water than the phone rang again. By now I should know to always look at the caller ID before I pick up, but lately I've gotten lazy. This time that gave me a problem.

"Hey, Gracie Lee. How're you doing?" That smooth Tennessee-tinged voice still made me want to drop the phone every time.

"Okay, Hal. What's up?"

"I need to talk to Ben about his ticket for Christmas, and what we're doing. Is he there?"

Where did the man *expect* his son to be this time of morning? He'd obviously forgotten so much of his own teenage life, and paid so little attention to Ben's that he had no clue. "Of course he's here. Sound asleep, but here."

"I'm not going to have time later to do this again and it's urgent. Can you get him awake enough to talk pretty quick?"

Oh, sure. Hal Harris could make my temper flare

more quickly than any man on the planet. Even Fernandez ran a distant second most of the time. Silent prayer was the only weapon powerful enough to deal with this without shrieking into the phone. After saying a fervent, silent prayer and taking a deep breath I felt calm enough to speak again. "I'll try, Hal, but I can't make any promises. He's a pretty sound sleeper."

There was a masculine noise of frustration on the other end of the phone. "You let him get away with anything, don't you? What's he doing in bed this late on a weekday?"

Still making my way to Ben's bedroom, I kept my temper as best I could. "First, let me remind you that it's several hours earlier in California than Memphis. And second, he's less than a week into his first break after a tough semester of college. If that's letting him 'get away with' anything, then deal with it because I'm fine with him sleeping in."

By then I was at Ben's door and I knocked harder than I'd planned to. Muffled, non-alert noises came from inside. "Ben? Your dad's on the phone. Do you want to talk?" I held the phone away from me so Hal didn't hear Ben's answer in case it was less than polite. While I'd cheerfully argue with Hal if only the two of us were involved, once Ben joined any situation I'd be pleasant and civil for his sake.

There was a groan and some thumping, and Ben opened the door just wide enough for me to see his rumpled hair, the one eye he had open and the saggy flannel pants he slept in. "I guess. Phone?" He held one hand out and I gave him the cordless handset and the door closed again. I went back to the kitchen to finish making coffee. It was still filling the carafe after brewing when there was a knock on the door.

"Hello. Come in," I told Ray. He stood at the doorway for a minute with his lidded paper cup and viewed me silently.

"Honest, if I knew it meant that much to you I would have agreed to drink your coffee," he said, sounding as if he meant it.

"What are you talking about?" This seemed to be my morning for male aggravation.

"You sound really ticked off at me and we haven't even talked yet." I waved away his concern and ushered him in.

"It's not you. Ben's dad called to talk to him a few minutes ago. I'm always unpleasant when I have to deal with Hal this early in the day." Of course I wasn't any better when I dealt with him later in the day, either.

Ray wore an expression of relief. "At least it wasn't me for a change."

My mood was already toast. "No, that will come in a few minutes when you tell me how wrong I am for suspecting anything."

He smiled weakly. "Aw, c'mon. Give me a chance here. I might even say you have a point."

I poured myself some coffee and sat down in the living room armchair, where I proceeded to tell Ray all about my encounter with Frankie Collins the day before. Of course I also had to give him the background

204

information on the kid from talking to his mom a couple times. I did leave out the little shoving match the two of us had at Christian Friends over a week ago. None of the rest of it impressed Fernandez, though.

By the time I finished he looked a bit sour and his coffee cup appeared to be mostly empty. He still waved away the offer of a refill. "Okay, you were right. I'm not going to tell you that you have a point. You have a son. What kind of stuff did he say at thirteen to sound tough?"

"Certainly he didn't offer threats of murder, at least not in my hearing."

"Now, look. If what you've told me is accurate, Frankie didn't threaten murder, either. There are lots of ways to 'take care of' somebody you don't like besides killing them. He's an angry kid who has a lot of good reasons to be angry. Let's leave it at that. Meanwhile I need to leave to prepare for court this afternoon."

"For this case or another one?"

Ray scowled. "This one. That hot-shot lawyer Ms. Adams got Seavers has made a motion to get the charges down to suspicions of manslaughter *and* get his client released on his own recognizance because he's such a low flight risk."

"Hey, you were the one who said you didn't think Matt was a murderer."

"That was before the evidence techs found his hand-print on an inside wall of that portable facility, right where you'd expect to see it if somebody pulled a heavy object, like a body, in there."

Lexy had been right in her assumptions, but this still made me mad. "Ray, that handprint could be from any time since they put that thing in the driveway. How can that one thing make you change your mind so radically?"

He gave me a look much like the one Ben usually gave me when he thought I was being denser than usual. It wasn't any more attractive or less annoying on Fernandez. "I'm not changing my mind that much. Seavers has been a person of interest ever since we knew how his girlfriend was involved. And now on top of everything else I have to worry about him getting out of jail and being back on the streets."

"As much as I want to see that happen, now I'm afraid he'll be in more danger out than in," I told him.

"Why? Because you heard a thirteen-year-old boy shooting off his mouth? Maybe you and that church group of yours can find a way to pray over both of them and make the situation go away." He pushed off the couch and left me to jump up and follow him to my own front door. "But if you'll excuse me, I still need to prepare for that hearing in Ventura."

He turned around when he got to the doorway. The speed of the motion almost made me run into him. "If you have any information like this again, please just call."

"As if I'd bother," I muttered after the door shut and I could hear him descending the stairs.

"Was that Detective Fernandez? What did he want?" Ben asked as he put the phone back in its cradle.

"Not much. What did your dad want?"

"To change the dates I'm going to be in Memphis, moving my flight up to Thursday instead of Friday. He, uh, wants me to meet somebody."

Oh, boy. The sheepish look on Ben's face gave me a clue as to what kind of "somebody" that might be. I just hoped that this time the "somebody" would be a little more serious, for Ben's sake, and maybe even be old enough that no one would mistake her for his older sister. Given Hal's taste in women, that last part might be too much to hope for. Not that I'd say that to Ben. "So does that work for you?"

"Pretty much," he said. "They cut into my planned time with Cai Li, but otherwise it's okay. You already planned for me to be gone anyway. I figure a day earlier wouldn't matter much."

"True." I'd be lonely without him, but technically it was Hal's year to have Ben for Christmas. If my ex-husband had a serious love interest at this point, he'd be even more anxious to start his time with Ben. Chances are good that Hal had actually changed the tickets last week sometime, before even asking his son. "How do you feel about all this?"

"What? Do you mean the changed date or spending Christmas with Dad and the Tennessee Grands?" When Ben put it that way, Hal's family sounded like a bad country band.

"Both. I imagine you were more anxious to go to Memphis before you had a girlfriend. And I know you enjoy spending time with your dad."

"A lot more than I like spending time with his parents sometimes." Ben sighed. "Do you think Grandma and Grandpa will ever get tired of showing each other up with money?"

"I'd like to think so, Ben, but I'm not sure that's going to happen. They were doing that before you were even born, so I certainly can't promise you that it's going to end anytime soon." It probably wouldn't end until one or the other of Hal's parents died. Even then whoever went first would be at a disadvantage because the last man—or woman—standing would have a chance at a better bequest to Hal or Ben. But for now I didn't want to dwell on all that stuff. "Do you think you'll shave before you fly out there?"

Ben grinned, making him look more like his father than ever. Whatever bad I could say about Hal, he'd been a very handsome young man and his son was no different. "Shave? No way. If I shaved, Grandma Lillian might ask me about my grades and school and if I have a job and all kinds of stuff like that. If I don't, all we'll talk about is this." He stroked his chin. So Ben was not only as handsome as his father, but he was even craftier. I'm going to have to keep an eye on that kid.

By four that afternoon I had gotten mighty antsy, wondering how the court hearing had gone for Matt. I hoped he wouldn't be spending this week before Christmas in jail. I didn't dare call Ray to find out, even though the information would be a matter of public record. None of the other Christian Friends were likely to know this soon, and I had no idea whether I could call the county courthouse and get information like that or not.

I'd cleaned up around the apartment and used up what excess energy I could by wrapping and mailing my mom's Christmas package. The line at the post office was incredible, and if the clerks were supposed to make us feel any better by wearing Santa hats, it was a wasted effort.

Once I left the post office I contemplated stopping by school to see if Linnette was in the bookstore and whether she knew anything about Matt. I drove in that general direction, since it wasn't much of a detour on my way home. Before I got there I passed another sign that made me pull into a different parking lot instead. Inside the building there I was likely to find somebody who could answer my question.

The Rancho Conejo satellite office of the *Ventura County Star* didn't have a lot of desks or equipment. Maybe a dozen cubicles ranged across the one fair-sized room, and it was hard to see how many of them were occupied. The receptionist looked like she hadn't been out of high school long, nor was she very concerned about security. When I told her I was looking for Sam Blankenship she stopped popping her gum while having a phone conversation long enough to point toward a corner cubicle and then went back to what she was doing.

The spot she'd pointed to didn't seem to be occupied, but I headed that way anyway, and I was in luck. Before

I found anything in my purse to leave a note for Sam with, he ambled across the open space between the cubicle maze.

"Hey, I was just thinking about you," he said with a smile. "Want to give me a quote for the incredibly small story I'm going to write about the guy charged with doing in the DB you found?"

"Maybe. What's a DB, and who is this guy?" I knew the answer to the second question, but not the first. Sam wore khakis and another one of his ties that I guessed came from a thrift store. At least he didn't shop the bargain bin in the thrift store anyway. And his white shirt, while it wasn't new, didn't have any stains or holes, either.

"Ah. Sometimes I forget that I don't always speak plain English any more. 'DB' means dead body. That's shorthand the cops use all the time, not in court or anything, but when they're talking to each other. And sometimes they use it when they talk to me. And the guy is . . . let me see—" he flipped out a notepad "—Matthew Seavers, age twenty-four, who just had a bail hearing that I covered at the county courthouse, for all the good it did me."

"Why, didn't anything happen?" My hopes sank a little at Sam's disappointed look.

"Not much. Nobody said anything that was worth a story, even if the guy did get released. His lawyer got the charges knocked down to suspicion of manslaughter and got the guy released to the custody of his employer, who vouched for him. But absolutely nobody was saying anything to anybody outside the courtroom."

I hated to tell Sam, but I thought that was as it should be. Ray wouldn't likely talk to him about any of this, and Brian couldn't have his client talking to anybody at this point. I was glad to hear that somebody at Leopold Plumbing thought enough of Matt to stand up in court for him. "So you think I'd have a comment on this?"

"Hey, it's possible. You found the body so maybe you have some ideas about who killed the guy. The cops must have thought this Seavers did it or they wouldn't have bothered to arrest him and hold him."

"Sam, I can't say anything you could use for publication. All I saw was Frank Collins after death. Nothing before that, and not much after that told me anything, either. Matt was on a crew that worked that remodeling project, but there had probably been a dozen guys around the site in the week before that, and I wouldn't have expected the week after Thanksgiving to be any different."

Sam blew out a gust of air that sounded like a horse snort. "Great. So I still have about a two-paragraph story with no details on anything." He looked down at his notes again. "Wonder if anything else that happened at the courthouse today is worth a couple inches. I may have to go back to working on a feature about the courthouse employees' contributions to Toys for Tots."

"Not as exciting as murder, but definitely a good cause. I know you'll do a nice job writing it up."

"Yeah, well, I better. They don't pay me the big bucks

to sit around." His wry grin commented more than his words on the "big bucks" Sam got as a reporter. I made a mental note to put together a tin of homemade cookies and bring it down to the newspaper office some time the end of the week. It sounded like the least I could do for a struggling journalist.

There weren't a lot of cars in the staff lot at school when I cruised by. I didn't see Linnette's anywhere, so I didn't bother stopping to check the bookstore. Once I got back home I realized that unlike most of my Southern California friends who had their cell phones charged, turned on and ready all the time, I'd been walking around all day with mine turned off. When I powered up there were messages waiting for me.

The answering machine message light blinked as well, and I debated which to check first. In the end it didn't matter much, because the only message that was worth listening to was repeated both places. "If you get to a phone before five-thirty, come join us for mochas at Charlie's," Linnette called out over what sounded like a crowd. She was probably standing in Charlie's when she left the message.

Charlie's was the independent coffee house closest to church, and the one we tended to visit at when school wasn't in session and my place of business didn't afford everybody somewhere to gather. I didn't even bother changing out of my errand-running jeans, but left a note for Ben and went straight back out to the car.

It was just early enough that rush hour traffic was still light, and I found Linnette and Lexy celebrating at a corner table. "Great, you got my message." My best friend patted the empty chair beside her. "We even saved you a place."

I ordered my own drink at the counter and splurged on whipped cream like my friends. "Brian seems to have been a very good choice as an attorney," I told Lexy as I sat down.

"I thought so. He called me as soon as they got out of court. Fred Chambers, the crew chief for Leopold, took Matt home with him tonight. He said this way he could keep an eye on him for a couple days."

"That makes sense. You look mighty festive," I told Lexy, admiring the red dress she wore.

"Office holiday lunch." She wrinkled her nose. "I could have thought of half a dozen ways I'd rather spend two hours today, but couldn't get out of it."

"What was so bad about it?" Linnette asked, always the Christian Friends leader.

Lexy surprised me by blinking away a couple tears. "Two different people that have been out on maternity leave joined us for lunch, both with these precious little babies in red-and-white stretchy suits gurgling in baby carriers."

Linnette patted her hand. "It's the roughest right around the holidays, isn't it? Everybody puts such an emphasis on family we forget how hard it is for those who don't have the family situation they want."

Lexy made a face. "And it's only going to get worse when we go to the family gatherings for the next two weeks and deal with the aunts and cousins who just have to ask the questions about why I'm *still* not pregnant."

It didn't seem fair that somebody as sweet and caring as Lexy had to go through that stuff. "Maybe we can make out a rotation chart so that Linnette and I can go with you to these things. There's nothing like the presence of a stranger to put a damper on the nosy questions."

Lexy gave a tremulous smile. "Thanks. I know you'd do it, too. I might take you up on it, too. In fact, maybe both of you could come the twenty-third for the buffet at Steve's mom's house. It will take more than one stranger to intimidate his aunt Rhonda."

At least we could laugh about things like that together, I thought. Maybe this could be a way for me to keep from spending the whole week of Christmas alone when Ben left. Once again hope, chocolate and friends saved a bad situation.

Chapter Eighteen

Since Ben now knew he would be leaving California Thursday to spend the holidays with his father, I didn't see much of him. Judging from the oddly wrapped packages that appeared under the tree some time during my busy Tuesday, he spent part of the time shopping. A great deal of it was spent with Cai Li, of course. This relationship must have been developing most of the semester, that or they had certainly clicked with each other quickly. They weren't to the point of finishing each others' sentences yet, and fortunately there were no inappropriate displays of affection in public, at least around me. But they just had that moony look gazing into each others' eyes that said "young and in love" to me.

The two of them spent a bit of time that evening at the apartment. I baked Christmas cookies while they played some goofy video game again. Finally at about nine Ben got on the computer, and a minute later gave a whoop.

"All right! I made the Dean's list. Pretty good for my first semester, huh?"

"Definitely. Let's see those grades." I put down the pan of cookies just out of the oven, and went into the living room where Ben had his class records still up on the screen. "So, maybe Philosophy of Religion wasn't as hard as you thought." He'd posted a B-plus in the class, and that was his lowest grade.

"Eh. Maybe it was as hard as I thought and I had some good study help. You want to call up your grades, too, Mom?"

"Sure. If you know my student ID number you can even do it for me, that or take the rest of the snicker-doodles off the baking sheet before they stick."

"There are warm cookies?" Ben looked at Cai Li. "Race you to the kitchen." With his long legs he beat her by several lengths and I could hear them laughing over the goodies there while I punched in the information to get the right screen up.

My grades were almost as good as Ben's. With only

having nine hours of grad work, a B in a three-hour class pushed me down to a 3.67, which still wasn't too shabby. I wondered if anybody out here at any of the arcades or kid-friendly places gave rewards for good grades. The hours Ben spent at Tilt in St. Louis playing games with those hard-won tokens for each A on his report card still conjure up pleasant memories. It made me consider asking the pair in the kitchen if they wanted to go someplace that served pizza and featured skee-ball machines just for old times' sake.

Still, I suspected that would get me eye rolls from both of them. Surely they felt too mature for such behavior. "Anybody for Showbiz Pizza?" I called out, waiting for the groans.

"Mom, you're so out of it. They haven't called it that in years. Maybe never in California," Ben hollered back. "Besides, they're closed by now. You know how Rancho Conejo rolls up the sidewalks by eight at night."

We settled for the local ice-cream parlor instead, with me buying. Since they were celebrating, both kids got the featured "kiddie" sundae. Personally it gave me a feeling of relief that these two weren't pushing for a more grown-up relationship right away. Any young woman who could eat bubble-gum ice cream with gummy worms and still claim to have a good time on a date was somebody Ben could bring home often.

After dessert the kids dropped me back off at the apartment to finish the rest of the cookie baking while they went to Cai Li's house to watch a movie. Once the baking and dishes were done I settled down to read my Bible study for the next morning. Since I was off this week, I'd agreed to go with Dot to the Wednesday morning women's study group. This time I wanted to be more than four verses ahead of the discussion in class.

It didn't take long to discover the next morning that almost everybody else had chosen this week before Christmas to slack off in preparation. I sat with Dot and she and I seemed to be the only ones who'd read the lesson in depth. Linnette focused on the conversations she'd had with her daughters the night before on the phone, cementing the fact that neither of them would be home for Christmas for more than a day. "And probably not even the same day, at that. This parenting adults stuff is hard. I mean, I want them to be independent people with their own plans and resources. . . ."

"But you'd also like them to be your girls during holidays and such," Dot finished as Linnette nodded in agreement.

Tracy Collins slid into the empty seat next to Dot, carrying a cup of coffee and looking less wan than she had in weeks. Instead she looked a bit irate. "So how do you keep kids from getting independent too quickly? Frankie pitched a fit this morning when I told him he had to get up and mind his sisters while I came here. You'd think I was torturing him or something."

Dot sighed. "A lot of teens go through that. They go through those phases where nothing is important except what their friends think."

"Yeah, and I don't like his friends. I wish he had different ones, preferably friends who didn't like headbanger music and T-shirts with rude sayings." I remembered being in Tracy's shoes in that regard just a few years ago. At least I'd had Hal to back me up from a distance. That and the assistance my mom gave me helped keep Ben on the right track. I kept my mouth shut right now, because I figured the last thing Tracy wanted was sympathy from me.

"Did he give you any particular reason for not wanting to watch the girls?" Dot asked. "Not that there's any good one, but maybe you could be prepared next time."

"He said he'd promised somebody he'd stay close to the phone and the computer. I threatened to take away his privileges on both if he didn't shape up, and that's when he totally lost it. He acted like whatever he was doing was a matter of life and death."

"So many things are when you're thirteen," Linnette said. "My girls were only a little older than that when their dad died, but it seemed like every crisis for about two years after that was blown way out of proportion. Maybe it was their way of using up the grief they hadn't spent when Tom died."

Tracy looked skeptical. "Maybe that's it. I don't know, though. Boys are so different. And since I was a little kid when most of my brothers went through being thirteen, I don't know if this is mostly normal stuff he's doing or way over the top."

"If my experience is any help, almost anything is possible from a boy that age, especially if you're raising him alone. Ben's dad was three states away and not real helpful when Ben was thirteen. I was basically on my own, and he was a handful."

Tracy's face softened. "Maybe I'm just expecting too much too soon. But I never know whether he's going to act way too mature for his age or younger than his four-year-old sister these days. I guess I didn't expect to get the preschooler behavior over just waking up early and watching the girls. It's like having Frank and his opinions all over again."

Ouch. I decided to let that slide without comment because I didn't have anything to say. It felt best to stick to teenagers. "It's a time to choose your battles. If you don't want to fight over everything you have to decide what the important things are and stick to those and ignore the rest. There were times when I felt like it would have needed a backhoe to clean Ben's room, but I could shut the door on it. I saved my breath for insisting he do his homework and be civil to his grandmother."

"The homework is a constant battle. It's a split decision on grandmas. He puts my mom down, but he makes nice with Grandma Collins because she slips him money and goodies that the girls don't get." Tracy's expression told me what she thought of her mother-in-law's behavior.

We'd gotten so far afield from the Bible study that it actually startled me when Helen Marshall, our study leader and the church secretary, got down to business, shushed us all and got into the lesson. Tracy and I didn't have any more time to talk, but her problems with Frank, Jr. were on my mind all morning.

When the study was over and I looked for her so we could talk more, she was gone. "Where'd Tracy go anyway?" I asked Dot. She usually kept track of everybody.

"I don't know. Her cell phone rang about twenty minutes into the study and she left the room and never came back. That's a shame because I was thinking about asking her if she wanted to go out to lunch with us."

"Us? Does that mean I'm included?"

"Certainly. And I'll ask Linnette since she's here, too. I was thinking about picking up Candace and Lucy for lunch someplace as a pre-holiday treat. Does that sound good?"

"Sure." Ben wouldn't be home for lunch on his last day here, I knew. He'd already told me he would have lunch with Cai Li and dinner with me and we'd have our Christmas gift exchange afterward. So I had nothing to hurry home for.

Linnette liked the idea of going, too, so we decided to leave her car in the lot and take Dot's and mine to Camarillo since I knew the way to the girls' place.

"Candace almost always has Wednesdays off, but I'm not sure about Lucy. With all the kids being off from school by now, she may be working extra hours at the theater," Dot said as we got into our cars and caravanned over to Rose House.

Lucy wasn't there when we arrived, but it wasn't

because she had to work. Kirsten looked sad when Dot told her our plans. "I'm afraid Lucy's gone. She complained of not feeling well yesterday afternoon, and when I called to tell Estella that, she came right over and hustled her sister out of here. She said all the excitement of everything going on was bad for Lucy and that she'd be better off at Estella's for a while. I don't know if that's true, as much time as she spends at the hospital. I hope she takes her to a doctor. Lucy looked like she was really hurting by the time they left here."

Dot sighed. "I guess that's Estella's decision to make. Too bad that Lucy won't be around for a while. I'd hoped we could take her to Christmas Eve services with us at the chapel. I imagine there's always next year, but she seems to have gotten comfortable at our church and I wanted to encourage that."

"I know. And Matt called here several times yesterday trying to reach her. Apparently Estella has changed her phone number and didn't give him the new one. I felt bad not being able to give it to him, but Ms. Perez told me it was an unlisted number and she didn't want it given out to *anyone,* especially not Matt." Kirsten didn't look like she agreed with that decision, but I knew she had to abide by it. "He and Lucy haven't gotten to see each other since he was arrested."

"That's a shame, but there's not much we can do about it. Let's get Candace and go to lunch," Dot said. She went down the hall and knocked on her daughter's bedroom door.

"Just a minute," Candace called. "Who is it?"

"It's your mother, come to take you to lunch."

"All right! But you'll have to open the door because my nails are wet." When Dot opened the door Candace sat at the desk in the room, manicure supplies out in front of her. "Green glitter polish for Christmas. Isn't it cool?" She waggled ten shiny nails.

Dot smiled. "Lovely, dear. Do you need to wait for them to dry before we go to lunch?"

"Not for long. I can put fast-drying stuff on them and we can go in five minutes. I hope it isn't real cold out there because I don't want to put a jacket on yet." Candace looked at me behind her mother and waved. "Hi, Gracie Lee. Hi, Linnette. Do you want to borrow my nail polish?"

The thought of wearing green glitter polish made me giggle and I could hear Linnette reacting the same way.

"Not this time, Candace. My son, Ben, would think I was acting like a teenager if I came home with that on my nails. Do you have any silver? Maybe I can borrow that for New Year's Eve." Ben wouldn't be home next week and I could get a little crazy. Besides, since I had no plans to ring in the New Year with anybody, doing a manicure with the girls might be the most exciting thing I did next week.

"Lucy has silver. I bet she'd let you borrow it," Candace said. "I miss Lucy already. It's not much fun without her here."

"Well, she should be back soon. Maybe after

Christmas she'll feel better and Estella will bring her back."

"I hope so. It's too quiet alone. And I'm tired of Tina's Barry Manilow Christmas album already." Since I would have gotten tired of that after the first listen, I could sympathize with her. We went out to the cars, discussing the merits of various local restaurants for lunch. I had to defer to the others, because I didn't know much about Camarillo.

In the end we all piled into Dot's car and had a good time at a Chinese place not far away. They all laughed at me because I got so excited when I saw the appetizer section of the menu.

"They have crab rangoon. This is the first place I've seen out here that has it."

Linnette gave me an odd look. "Is it something special?"

"Yeah. They're delicious. Think of fried wontons with cream cheese and crab in them instead of meat. In St. Louis it's as easy to get as toasted ravioli."

Linnette started to say something but Dot laughingly waved her off. "Don't get her started on that. She described it to me once and it sounds revolting."

I shrugged. "Suit yourself. Maybe it's an acquired taste. There's nothing to compare it to in California so I don't try."

Now I felt really excited about lunch. I decided to get the appetizer instead of a lunch special. That meant I'd miss the cool sectioned rectangular dish lunch came in out here, almost as large as a cafeteria tray. The food on them is different, too; the first time I ordered egg foo yung in California it seemed to have been prepared inside out. By now I've gotten used to all the differences except the lack of crab rangoon.

Everybody ordered and we chatted and drank hot tea while we waited for the food to come. Dot asked Linnette if she knew where Tracy went. "Not a clue. She got a call and vanished. I wonder if she ever got in touch with either of the accountants Pastor George recommended."

"There's a girl with a lot of problems," Dot said. "I hope she doesn't lose the house."

"Why would that happen?" Linnette asked. "All she has to do is straighten out the business books and wait for Frank's insurance to pay out."

"That will cover the house payment, but what will she and those three kids do for living expenses now that Frank's gone? Her limited skills aren't going to do enough." Dot looked troubled, and I could see that the discussion was bothering Candace as well. She had her mom's soft heart for people.

Linnette gave Dot an odd look. "You're kidding, right? Frank Collins is probably worth a lot more dead than alive. Tracy shouldn't have anything to worry about."

Now I felt confused, too. "What do you mean? She's been acting like she didn't know where her next penny was coming from."

"That's odd. Frank owned his contracting company, didn't he?"

"For what it was worth. He was always one step away from losing everything the way he stiffed his suppliers and his subcontractors." Dot picked up her teacup as if she wanted to drown a bad taste in her mouth.

"Well, that's over now. To have his contractor's license as a sole operator, the state and his subs would have made him carry insurance to protect the business if he died. It would have to be in an amount big enough to cover any debts the business held, and pay a healthy sum afterward."

This had me thinking in a way that made it hard to enjoy the hot, crispy crab rangoon that came to the table just then. I imagine it was actually as good as Missouri crab rangoon, but I got too busy mulling over things in my mind to enjoy it.

While we drove Candace back to Rose House, she and Dot discussed the rest of the week. "Maybe you can come get me after I get off of work tomorrow night. It's so quiet without Lucy. I'd rather be at your house with my Dixie dog and you and Daddy."

"That sounds like a good idea. If you're there you can keep your father from sneaking Dixie and Hondo Christmas cookies." The mental picture of Candace as the cookie police made me grin in the back seat. It sounded like a job she could really warm up to.

When we got back to Rose House Kirsten was standing on the front porch. Her forehead was creased with worry. "Good, you're back. Something weird is going on and I'm trying to decide whether to call the police."

"What happened?" The feelings of unease that I'd had at lunch came roaring back.

"Estella Perez called here about ten minutes ago in a panic. She demanded that I tell her where her sister was, that she had to have her back right away because of a medical emergency. She was sure that Lucy had come here."

Dot looked as worried as Kirsten. "How could Lucy have gotten from her sister's house to here? It's got to be ten miles."

"And Lucy's sick besides. When Estella took her home with her she looked like she was coming down with the flu or something."

"Was she feverish?" One of my growing concerns today made me ask the question even though Linnette and Dot looked at me strangely.

"Flushed, maybe but it was more her complaint that she just hurt all over that made me think she was getting something nasty," Kirsten said. "But I still can't understand how her sister could think she made it all the way here."

Candace had been silent through our conversation but now she gave a long low sound that was almost a moan. "I promised not to tell but now I've got to tell. Matt has a motorcycle. He came by Lucy's work with it one day. I bet he found her and took her away on his motorcycle."

Dot looked at Candace in dismay. "Call the police, Kirsten. In fact, let Gracie Lee give you the direct number for Ray Fernandez. I think he will want to hear all this."

Dot was right, but my biggest concern was finding Lucy right now. If my suspicions were right the last thing she needed was a trip on the back of a motorcycle.

Chapter Nineteen

Dot knew Estella's address and had no problems, since Lucy was missing, in giving it to me. She and Kirsten pretty much figured that confidentiality was out the window at this point. I knew that if Ray thought we were heading to Estella's he would order us away, so I had Kirsten make the call to him. She had the most complete information anyway. We left Lucy there with her and drove back to Rancho Conejo.

"Knowing that Matt has access to a vehicle changes everything. Maybe we've been too quick to defend him," Linnette said.

"I hope not. I still don't think that Matt having a motorcycle means he is a murderer. In fact I think it could explain why he's looked so uncomfortable all along. He wasn't supposed to have a vehicle."

"We can pray you're right, Gracie Lee." After that we were mostly silent on the quick drive. Since the church parking lot wasn't all that far from the address Dot gave me, I dropped Linnette off at her car. "Are you sure you won't just join me and go home? It's probably the smartest thing to do," she said as she got out of my car.

"I know it's the smartest, but I'm not going to leave Dot by herself over there and she insisted on going." I also needed to see this through to a conclusion somehow, and had the feeling that might happen very soon.

I pulled up right behind Dot, who was standing by her car. Ray hadn't arrived yet. "Do we wait here or go knock on the door?" Dot asked.

"I don't know. We don't want to spook her, but she shouldn't leave, either. Maybe we can offer to help look for Lucy."

We agreed on that and went to Estella's front door. She nearly slammed it in our faces once she saw who stood there outside her small ranch-style house. It looked like it could be one her family had lived in before the accident that changed all their lives. Small and tidy, it could have used a coat of paint over the aging stucco.

"What do you want? This really isn't a good time for a visit right now," she said, glaring.

"We thought we'd offer to help you find Lucy."

She looked startled. "How do you know about that? I haven't told anybody but Kirsten."

"We took Candace out to lunch today," I told her. "We got back to Rose House just after your phone call when Kirsten was trying to decide whether to call the police."

"She didn't call the police! This isn't a police matter."

"Don't you think it's too late to decide that?" I asked softly. "You know we need to find your sister quickly before she loses a lot of blood."

Estella's shoulders slumped. "How did you figure it out? Was it that obvious?"

"No, not really. I just heard and saw things with a different perspective than anybody else." I could hear a car door slam behind us and footsteps on the brick walk leading to the house.

Ray growled a couple words in Spanish that I was sure weren't in the beginner's book, even in an adult ed class. "Mrs. Morgan, how did she involve you in this?" he asked. "Neither of you belong here."

Estella Perez stood straighter and her chin jutted out. "I'm glad they're here. In fact, Detective Fernandez, I don't think I'll agree to talk to you inside my house unless they stay." Judging from Ray's expression it was the last thing he expected to hear.

Ten minutes later we sat in Estella's living room, grouped on a sofa and love seat that had been new about the time Reagan left the White House.

"Am I the only one taken by surprise by all this?" he asked, waving a hand over the scene.

"Not totally. I thought about it early on, but pretty much dismissed the idea when Estella backed her sister up about not being able to have babies."

"Am I going to face criminal charges?" Estella wasn't the confident woman we'd seen before. She looked worn and far older than thirty.

"We'll have to talk about that later. It depends on how much you've concealed. Did you know that Seavers had a motorcycle?"

Estella sighed. "It's not a cycle, it's only a scooter. Just an old beat-up Vespa that's barely street legal. I made Lucy promise not to ever ride it with him when she told me about it."

"Still, that changes the entire focus of our investigation into Frank Collins's murder. Even if you don't face any charges regarding your sister, there will probably be some for withholding information during a murder investigation." Ray looked tired and even older than Estella. "Do you know the license plate number of the scooter?"

Estella shook her head. "I haven't ever seen it myself. But I bet if you ask my neighbors you'll find out that it was here in the twenty minutes I was gone to the grocery store at noon. I shouldn't have risked leaving her alone but she was asleep and I'd run out of several things I had to have."

"I hope your mistakes don't cost your sister her life." Ray looked like he was going to keep on with his lecture but his cell phone rang in his jacket pocket. "Fernandez." He listened for a few moments and asked a couple questions, nodding when he got the answers. Closing the phone and putting it back in his pocket, he scowled.

"That was Jeannie, reporting in after making phone calls. Seavers is not on the construction site like he should be. When his boss went to lunch Seavers got a phone call and he split. So much for Chambers being responsible for him."

"Now what do you do?" Estella looked even more worried than she had before.

"We put a description of Seavers, the motor scooter and your sister out to all black-and-white units and the citizen patrols. And we spread out through the neighborhood from here looking for them."

He gave me a sharp look. "And that 'we' I'm talking about refers to the county sheriff's department, not the other people in this room. Got it?"

"I hear you, Ray. Am I at least allowed to drive home?"

He sighed. "Make it a very direct route, Gracie Lee. I don't want you in trouble again."

Ray made more phone calls posting the information on Lucy, Matt and the scooter with a dispatcher. He cautioned Estella not to leave the area. "In fact, I'd recommend you stay right here in case your sister comes back. If that happens, call 911 first and me second."

Estella agreed that she would, and we went out to our cars. "Do you think he'll follow us to make sure we go straight home?" Dot asked me quietly.

"I wouldn't put it past him. But if we go in two different directions he can only follow one of us. Don't you have to go back and get Candace?"

Dot's eyes twinkled. "Actually, I do. Should I tell Detective Fernandez that?"

"It would explain why we aren't going the same way. That way he won't think right away that we're ignoring his directions." Dot went over to Ray's unmarked unit and stood by the driver's side door until he opened the window a bit. While she talked to him, I got in my car and headed in the general direction of my apartment. I didn't use the most direct route possible, but I didn't stray much, either. I have to admit I was driving rather slowly, using a few more side streets than usual and keeping an eye out for a blue motor scooter.

Down a street that seemed familiar for a reason I couldn't quite grasp, in the middle of the block in front of a house that looked much like its neighbors with its tan stucco front, clay tile roof and a straggly looking olive tree out front, I almost missed it. Close to the side of the house behind a rusting iron gate, parked on one of those swaths of concrete they called RV pads out here, there was a blue scooter. I drove past the house and parked two down, coming back on foot to investigate.

How common was a blue Vespa? I didn't want to call the police if this was somebody else's motor scooter. I could only imagine how Ray would react if several black-and-whites screamed up to this house only to find some poor, unsuspecting scooter owner. The gate stood slightly ajar, so I wasn't really trespassing by walking through, was I? A touch of the scooter told me it was still warm. If it wasn't Matt's, then somebody else had been out for a ride on a similar scooter.

I heard a woman's voice from the back of the house. She was yelling at someone. "Frankie, no! Where did you get that? Put it down." The name was familiar and so was the voice. When I looked around the corner of the house, Tracy Collins stood over the prone form of Matt Seavers. Between them on the ground lay a silver aluminum baseball bat. That frightened me, but what was even more frightening was Frankie, a gun in his hand, pointing it at his own mother.

Before anyone saw me I pulled back to the side of the house. For once I decided to follow Ray's advice. I pulled out my cell phone and called 911. It was only when the operator answered that I realized I didn't know the street address. Praying that it was on the front of the house, I got there as quickly and quietly as I could. One of the faded metal numbers hung by only one nail, but they were all there. I gave the address to the operator and told her to relay the message to Ray as well. I hadn't ever memorized his phone number, something that I promised myself I'd do at the next opportunity.

Going back to the corner of the house, the tableaux in front of me hadn't changed. Matt lay stretched on the concrete, not moving. Tracy, talking feverishly, stood very still while her son pointed a gun at her.

Frankie interrupted her. "You hit him with that bat before he even said anything, Mom. Why? What's going on?"

"I was protecting you and your sisters. Just like I have been all along. He's a bad man, Frankie. He's the one who killed your father."

"Is that why you called him on the phone and told him he had to come here or you'd turn him in to the police?" Frankie's slender shoulders trembled so that I could see the movement from twenty feet away. "I heard you call. And I heard the other call to Uncle Mike, the one where you told him that with Dad's insurance you could send all of us through college. I don't think he killed Dad, not unless you paid him to do it." Frankie choked out the last few words on the ragged note of a kid whose voice was changing almost as fast as his world.

"That's ridiculous. He's the one the police arrested. Either shoot him or put down the gun." Tracy took a step toward her son, who waved the gun at her and gave a strangled cry.

I could hear the slight sound of well-tuned cars on the street in front, and several car doors opening. Then the gate squealed open and I pressed my back against the rough stucco of the house to let three uniformed officers past. They were all shouting as they rounded the corner. "Police. Put the gun down. Don't shoot." Ray charged just steps behind them and I held my breath.

"Thank heavens you're here," I heard Tracy say in a loud voice. "This man tried to attack me and my family. He said something about finishing what he started. He was like a maniac."

"That's not true!" Frankie shouted. "He didn't say anything. You hit him with a bat. You killed him!"

"Whatever happened, holding that gun in front of four armed police officers won't help anything, son. We'll sort things out. You just put the gun down." Ray's voice was amazingly even and calm. I couldn't bear to look around the corner and see what was happening. Instead I prayed, fervently, for everybody involved. "Come on now. Put your arm down and take your finger away from the trigger. Nobody wants to shoot or get shot here."

A clatter of something heavy on concrete relieved me

so much I couldn't stand upright any more. The RV pad felt cool beneath me as I sat there long enough to draw several breaths. Then I got up on shaky legs and finally looked to see what was going on. Tracy, protesting loudly, was being restrained by one of the officers, while Frankie had been dragged away from where the gun lay on the pavement and pressed against the back wall of the house by another officer.

"Why are you doing this? I'm the victim here," Tracy shrieked. "My son is hysterical. He doesn't understand what he's saying. That man threatened to kill us!"

"That's not what happened," I said. "At least it isn't what Frankie said he heard and saw."

Ray knelt beside Matt's body where the young man still lay in the same position I'd seen him in ten minutes ago. He looked up at Tracy. "We'll know soon enough what really happened here. Seavers is still alive, even though somebody tried to brain him with this baseball bat. Once he's treated at the hospital we'll know who's telling the truth."

The officer who wasn't restraining anybody pulled a crackling radio off her belt and called for an ambulance. Tracy sat in an Adirondack chair on the patio, breathing hard and glaring at everyone now. Ray took a step closer to her. "I don't know whose story is true here, but you can help things by telling me the truth on one issue, Ms. Collins. When Seavers got here, was he alone?"

At first Tracy said nothing. She seemed to be weighing her options. "Of course he was alone," she spat out finally. "What would you expect from somebody threatening a defenseless woman and three little kids?"

"I'm no little kid," Frankie said. "And I know what I heard. That guy didn't threaten anybody."

He and his mother stayed silent after that, their energies spent. In a few minutes an ambulance crew was in the driveway, and minutes later Matt's inert form got loaded on a gurney and the crew left with the siren wailing.

Once they left Ray looked over and seemed to really see me for the first time. "I should find something to charge you with over this. I told you to go straight home."

"Yes, and if I had Matt Seavers would be dead right now and no one would ever know that he didn't kill Frank Collins."

"I wouldn't be so sure of that last part. You haven't been privy to the *whole* investigation here, Ms. Harris. No matter what, we still have one big problem."

"Lucy's still missing."

"Still missing, probably in bad shape physically, and nobody seems to have a clue where she could be."

"Not necessarily. After the last hour and seeing everything I've seen, I have an idea where she might be."

Ray looked at me with more skepticism than I'd seen him display in weeks. "Then you're coming with me. And if by some chance you're actually right, I'll forget what I said about charges."

"I hope so. Can you drive to where we're going? I don't think I'm capable yet." Ray barked a couple of orders at the uniformed officers and led me to his car in a less-than-gentle fashion.

When I told him where to go, he shook his head. "And I had such high hopes we could still be friends," he said.

"Just get there," I told him, getting into the car and fastening my seat belt. I hadn't ever ridden with Fernandez, but I suspected it would be a bumpy ride.

The lot at Conejo Community Chapel looked nearly deserted. Even Pastor George's parking spot was empty. Ray pulled up close to the church and looked at me. "Are you sure about this?"

"Not certain, but it just feels right. Let's go in and see."

The door to the hallway between the church itself and the classrooms was unlocked. In the hallway bright children's drawings of mangers and shepherds and angels festooned with glitter lined the walls, reminding me of what season it was. My throat tightened as I walked toward the church, silently praying that my intuition was right.

"I don't think—" Ray began when I grabbed his arm to silence him. Maybe he couldn't hear it, but I could hear the high, thin wail of a very young baby and it seemed to be coming from the sanctuary. As a mother I'd have to say that no matter how long it's been since you've heard that sound it demands your attention when you hear it again. How anybody can ignore that urgency is beyond my understanding.

When I pushed open the back door of the sanctuary it was easy to hear that it was truly a baby crying that I'd heard. From down the hallway I could convince myself that it might be an older child somewhere with his or her mom, but in this large open space the sound was unmistakable. Standing in the center aisle between the rows of chairs was Lucy Perez, holding a blanket-wrapped bundle. Even though it was what I'd hoped for, the sight stunned me enough to root me to the spot for over a minute, watching her awkwardly jiggle the wailing newborn.

"We don't want to startle her," Ray said in a voice not much louder than a whisper. I nodded, walking up the aisle quietly.

A few feet up I called Lucy's name just loudly enough for her to hear me over the infant's cries. She turned to me, and her dark eyes appeared clouded with confusion. "Hi. You're Candace's mom's friend."

"That's right. My name's Gracie Lee. Who do you have there?" Lucy still wore her usual somewhat-shapeless velour sweats, but now she looked more slender than she had the last time I saw her.

"I don't know her name. I'm not even sure where she came from. Estella took me home with her because I was real sick. Once I got to her house I felt worse. My back hurt and I had a tummy ache and I felt like throwing up."

That all sounded like a bad case of the flu or a normal course of labor. I tried to keep my voice level while I talked to Lucy, who wasn't paying any attention to Ray standing at the back doors of the sanctuary. "Then what happened?"

"She gave me something that made me . . . sleepy." Lucy looked like that wasn't really the word to describe what she'd felt. She wasn't quite weaving on her feet, but she didn't look far from it. "What day is it?"

"Wednesday." She looked ready to wilt and I had to do something. "Do you want to hand the baby to me? Maybe I can get her to stop crying."

The baby in my arms was very new. Red and wrinkled with eyes squinched tightly shut as she cried, she couldn't be more than a day old. She had good healthy lungs, though. "How did you get here, Lucy?"

"I walked. Estella's house is close to here."

I marveled at her ability to get from one place to another drugged and in such difficult circumstances. "So what made you take a walk with the baby?"

Lucy looked as if she was still piecing that together for herself. "I woke up and nobody was there except me. And this baby. That was a problem."

"Yes, I guess it was. So you decided to find somebody to help you with the problem?" My jiggling the infant wasn't having a real calming effect on her. I thought of the baby as "her" because Lucy said she was. The wails were a little quieter now, but definitely not stopped.

"Sort of." Lucy had a faint smile that made her look even more otherworldly than she had before. "I thought about what Candace said. I remembered about Jesus and problems, so I took her here. Maybe Jesus can help find her mommy."

The baby latched on to the knuckle I stroked across her tiny mouth, quieting while she sucked furiously. The pressure was incredible and stirred something deep inside me. "Lucy, this may be hard for you to understand, but I think this is *your* baby."

Her eyes got huge. "I can't have a baby. I'm not married. Only married people have babies."

Something more dawned on me then. "Is that why you said you were like Candace and couldn't have babies? Because you aren't married?"

She still looked hazy, but she nodded in answer. "Sure. Frank was married. He could have a baby. Do you think because he was married and he did stuff to me I could have this baby?"

This wasn't the time to go into the complexities of all this with Lucy, but I had to give her some answer.

"That could be what happened." The baby started to wail again and I knew we needed help that Jesus couldn't provide alone. Ray must have recognized that, too, because it was only a few minutes before I saw my second ambulance crew of the day.

One of the paramedics that responded looked familiar to me. Her dark blue shirt said "Anna" on the front, and I was pretty sure she'd been on at least one of the runs that had taken me from Edna's house to the nearest hospital last spring. While the ambulance units didn't carry baby formula as a matter of procedure, they did apparently carry glucose solution and soon the baby was working on a bottle of that.

I tried to explain what I knew to Anna and her partner

in as quiet a voice as possible. The other crewman, whose shirt said "Dave" on the front and EMT on the back, had talked Lucy into lying on a gurney they'd rolled into the sanctuary. Ray's 911 call had apparently gotten a little garbled and these two responded to what they thought was a birth happening in the Conejo Community Chapel sanctuary.

Anna looked relieved that she didn't have to help deliver a baby. She seemed at a loss listening to Lucy.

"Estella always tells me when she goes someplace. But today I woke up and she was gone. And there was this baby." She looked down at the bottle Anna had given her and the blanket-wrapped babe in her arms sucking at the bottle. "Gracie Lee said I might be her mommy. Do you think that's true?"

This presented another challenge for Anna. "It sure looks like it. Don't you remember having her?"

"I don't remember anything after yesterday afternoon. Estella said I was real sick. She gave me stuff that made me sleepy. I kind of remember hurting a lot." Lucy paused to watch the baby, then looked up again.

"Do you know where Matt is? He called me at my house and said he got out of jail. But then Estella took me with her and he didn't call anymore, and he didn't come visit me."

Ray sighed. "Maybe we can find your sister and Matt for you. Before that, I think you need to go to the hospital so they can see how sick you are." He patted her shoulder farthest from the baby and looked over at

Anna. "Okay, she's all yours now. I'll call in later to see how she is."

"Fine. I think she's basically all right but we'll leave the final decision on that to the docs." Anna called to her partner and they carefully started the process of getting Lucy and the baby into the ambulance.

As they rolled down the main aisle of the church, Helen came into the sanctuary. "What on earth is happening here? We just got back from lunch and there's an ambulance in the parking lot."

"Do you want to tell her, or should I? Either way we've both got plenty to do."

Ray smiled for the first time this afternoon. "You tell her and I'll go get in my car. Somebody has to call Estella and follow that ambulance to the hospital."

Halfway through explaining the convoluted afternoon to Helen, interrupted by Pastor George coming in and needing explanation as well, I realized I needed a favor from one of them. My car was still on the street in front of Frank Collins's house. And I needed to get home to have Christmas with Ben. He would never believe how I spent my afternoon.

Chapter Twenty

Ben and I ended up having carryout pizza for our Christmas celebration dinner and opened our presents about eleven that evening. He reacted every bit as badly to my stories of the afternoon as I expected him to. "Are you sure I can leave you on your own and go to Tennessee?" he asked after I told him what happened, sounding more like the parent than the college kid. It made me glad I hadn't talked to my mother yet.

"I'm sure. All the excitement is over now and I won't get into any more trouble. If you like I'll call and check in with you every afternoon at three."

He grinned at me then. "You don't need to do that, Mom. You can just e-mail every day and report. I'm bringing my laptop and Dad has a wireless network."

"Good thing. If he didn't those phone bills from Memphis to Newbury Park would add up in a week's time." He didn't bother arguing with me on that point. Maybe the kid really is maturing.

LAX the next morning was an absolute zoo. It's what I expected the week before Christmas, but *expecting* that kind of mass of humanity and experiencing it are two different things. I insisted on finding a space in the parking garage and walking Ben as far into the terminal as possible, which wasn't very far. He used one of the self-serve machines to get his boarding pass, shouldered his luggage and there he was, ready to go through security. I wondered how he could really pack for a week in a backpack and a small duffel, but he had been old enough to manage his own packing for quite a few years now, so I didn't ask.

The lump in my throat from hugging him goodbye and watching him go lasted at least back to the 101. That's saying something, because the interchange of the 405 freeway and the 101 is a place where I've never seen a clear stretch of road, even the time I drove it at two in the morning. Los Angeles's love affair with cars means there is *always* traffic on the major roadways.

Things thinned out considerably when I got closer to Rancho Conejo. By the time I crossed the Ventura County line I could go fifty miles an hour instead of crawling at twenty. When I had almost reached the exit to turn off for home my cell phone rang. "You up for lunch at *Mi Familia*?" a familiar voice asked. "I want to talk about yesterday some more."

"Sure, as long as you agree to keep your word about not hitting me with charges," I told Fernandez.

"Gracie Lee, have I ever lied to you?"

"Depends on what you call lying. You certainly haven't told the full truth every time we've talked."

There was a sigh on the other end of the phone. "Let's postpone that argument until we're face-to-face. Eleven forty-five okay? I want to beat the rush."

I agreed on the time and went home to touch up my makeup and add a light cotton Christmas sweater over my jeans and shirt. Driving Ben to LAX and lunching with Ray Fernandez required two rather different "looks" as far as I was concerned.

I pulled into the restaurant parking lot next to Ray's unmarked unit. Since he was just getting out of the car I couldn't be accused of being late. He looked sharp as ever in his workday uniform of white shirt, jeans and a sport coat. Today he'd even added a tie that looked as Christmas oriented as I could expect from him. It featured the Grinch, of course.

He insisted on picking up the tab for lunch. "We can

call this one departmental business as long as we don't go wild." I wasn't sure how one would go wild at *Mi Familia* with the average lunch running about six bucks. That was what my cheese enchilada special ran, and Ray's carnitas burrito was about the same.

"Think the department will pop for an orange soda, too? I don't want to push the limit."

"Definitely. You could even have the high-end one imported from Mexico in a glass bottle." His smile was positively lupine today. It was a look that made me glad that I was on the right side of this man of the law.

We settled at a table and waited for Luis to call our order. While we waited we caught each other up on the last twenty-four hours. "Tell me you didn't file charges against Estella Perez." Personally I thought she had enough problems facing her without legal trouble, but I wasn't sure how the system would look at her actions.

"No charges, but she'll probably be up for disciplinary action at the hospital. She may have 'borrowed' some of the supplies she used to deliver Lucy's baby. And if nothing else, she acted in a highly unethical manner the way she did things."

"How long had she known Lucy was pregnant? And what did she use to sedate her so that she didn't remember anything but still had a healthy baby?"

"She figured out her sister's condition a while ago, and didn't tell her because she didn't think Lucy could handle the information. I think Estella wanted the baby so much herself that she decided to keep things quiet until the baby was born. Maybe she even thought she could get away with this and somehow present the baby as one she'd adopted or something." Ray looked puzzled by that.

"Some women want a child so badly they'll do anything to get one." I thought of the sorrow in Lexy's voice when she told her stories at Christian Friends. While she wouldn't do what Estella had done, she would certainly go to great lengths to have a baby. "So what about the drugs?"

Luis called out that our food was ready and Ray stood up to go get the tray. "She tried to explain it to me, but I don't have a lot of medical knowledge," he said over his shoulder. "Apparently it's a modern version of something called 'twilight sleep.' She said my mother could probably explain it."

"Anybody your mom's age, or mine, could explain it," I told him when he came back with the laden tray. "The old stuff was morphine and something else that took away pain, but most of all made you forget all about it afterward. I've heard of dentists using something like it now for phobic patients." I didn't add that I came close to falling in that category myself and that's why I knew about the stuff. No reason to share my deepest secrets with the homicide detective, even if he was buying me lunch.

We ate in silence for a few minutes. Then I couldn't resist asking a few more. "How are Lucy and the baby doing? And what about Matt? I'm sure charges were dropped against him, but does he even *know* that yet?"

"Lucy's good. They're keeping her and her daughter

in the hospital another day or two, mainly to give her some parent education. I talked to somebody from Children and Family Services who seems to think that with a lot of support she could keep the baby. If she and Estella could come to an understanding, the two of them would do a fine job together raising her."

I tried not to huff. "Either I've got to stop asking more than one question at once or you've got to get better with answers. Which is it going to be?"

"It better be you with the questions, because I'm so used to keeping my answers to myself that retraining me now would be near impossible." The man had such a charming demeanor when he wanted to.

"Is Matt going to be okay? And will he get charged for driving without a license?"

"Once he's all right physically, he'll face some moving violation stuff. We'll try to keep it as light as possible but we can't ignore it totally. Of course if he'd told me about the scooter in the first place I probably wouldn't have liked him for the murder for so long. The way he was acting, I figured I had a contract killer on my hands."

"So you suspected Tracy of killing her husband?"

"I couldn't rule her out," Ray said. "She had the most to gain from having him dead. He was a bad, dishonest businessman and a lousy husband. With him gone, she profited financially *and* got rid of a guy her family had hated for years. I still thought Matt pulled the trigger for her, though."

"What changed your mind?" With Ray doing a lot of

the talking I had managed to polish off most of my lunch. I was beginning to think that maybe this time I'd spring for dessert.

"A couple things put me on another path. There's no proof anywhere that Matt Seavers has any money outside his job on the plumbing crew. And one of the unidentified prints on the inside of the portable facility where Collins was found matched a partial on the gun, and both belong to Tracy Collins."

"She could argue that she'd touched the gun another time, since her husband owned it, but I've never seen her at the job site."

"Exactly. She's lawyered up for now and we won't be getting any more information out of her. I hope she will confess and plea bargain down for the sake of her kids and not go through a trial, but who knows. She supposedly did all this for them, and now her husband's mother and one of her own brothers will squabble for years over custody while she's behind bars."

It was a sad situation to think of, and it pretty much killed my appetite for dessert. When we finished lunch and got ready to leave, I saw a sign on the back wall that said the restaurant would be open at 7:00 a.m. on Christmas Eve so that people could pick up tamales.

"Do you get yours here?" I asked, motioning to the sign. "I've been really tempted to learn how to make them. It's such a California thing."

"Yeah and it takes a small army. No, I don't buy tamales at Christmas. I go to my mother's house Christmas Eve and she'd skin me alive if I ate tamales anywhere but at her table."

"Do you think she'd welcome an extra pair of hands in the small army?"

Ray threw back his head in laughter. "You have got to be kidding. I wouldn't bring a woman into that lion's den on Christmas Eve unless we had dated at least six months. Even then, I'd have to be sure she could hold her own almost anywhere."

He gave me a speculative look as we left the restaurant. "Now I could see you holding your own, even in my mother's kitchen. Do you think if we started going out now we could talk about tamales next Christmas?"

The thought of what that meant made me stop dead in the parking lot. "Only if we talked about a lot of other things first. Like our coming to an understanding on issues of faith, because I won't get serious about another man who isn't a Christian." After the pain I'd already had in my life from relationships, I didn't want more pain of a type I could avoid.

He put his hands on my shoulders and pulled me closer. There was still space between us, but it had just narrowed considerably. "Gracie Lee, you know that even a week ago I would have turned that down flat. But I've seen what your faith and your trust or intuition or whatever you want to call it, can actually do. And I'm willing to at least give it a deeper look."

"So do you want to go to church with me Christmas Eve?" I always pushed this man's limits. Why should now be any different?

"Not this time. I really do have to spend the evening

at my mom's on pain of death. How about the Sunday after Christmas?"

"You've got a deal." I meant it whole-heartedly. I just didn't expect him to seal our deal with a kiss. It was brief, the kind of first kiss I'd expect from somebody standing in a parking lot with people coming and going. But brief didn't mean that it wasn't also mighty fine. Playing back that kiss in my head had me grinning like a fool the rest of the day.

Christmas Eve services at Conejo Community Chapel fulfilled all my expectations. I hadn't been here last year for this season and this year I was more than ready for Christmas to come. For a lot of reasons I avoided the kid-heavy services early in the evening, although watching six-year-olds go off like skyrockets from Christmas excitement did have its appeal. Tonight I wanted something a little more quiet and thoughtful.

For me the most meaningful service at Christmas is held late at night, with carols and candlelight, so that's the one I chose. My memories of Granny Jo's church in Missouri make me want peace at Christmas and maybe a dusting of snow. Actually, I'm fine without the snow as long as I get the peace.

Before setting out for church I'd talked to Ben. It must have been midnight in Memphis when he called, but it didn't surprise me he was up and wanted to talk. We'd e-mailed and instant messaged back and forth more than once, but hadn't really talked to each other since he left California. "So how's the weather? Did you get a white Christmas?"

"Only if you count ice storms. It's really cool to drive on if you're in a parking lot, though. Dad's SUV can do donuts like you wouldn't believe." There was a pause while Ben considered what he'd just told me. "We were all wearing our seat belts, though."

Great. As if that was supposed to calm me down a whole bunch. Still, it was Christmas and I wasn't going to nag at him. "So, how is the somebody Dad wanted you to meet?"

"Okay. I think she's awful young for him. She might be thirty, maybe, but not any older. And I hate to tell you this, but he gave her a ring tonight at dinner."

Oh, boy. Hal had gone through several semi-serious relationships since our divorce over fifteen years ago, but never remarried. "Wow. Sounds like big stuff."

"But wait, there's more." Ben sounded like those awful pitchmen on late-night TV. "How would you feel about Dad moving to California?"

"Where in California?" It's a big state. There might be room for both of us given enough distance.

"Hmm. Where would somebody live who was going to UC-Santa Barbara? I think that's where Nicole said her school program is."

"Santa Barbara?" I tried not to sound as ill as I suddenly felt. "That's only forty miles north of here." And housing prices there meant I could look forward to being in the same county with my ex-husband and his beautiful, young fiancée. I knew Hal well enough to know that not only would she be young, but she'd be beautiful as well. He wouldn't have things any other way.

My first thoughts were unpleasant, but I held my tongue. Again, this was Christmas and I was talking to my son. For him this might be good news, having his parents close enough that visiting Dad didn't mean a cross-country flight.

"So how's Cai Li?" It felt like time to change the subject.

"Okay. Did you already go to church tonight?"

"Not yet," I told him, wondering if that was the right answer or not.

It must have been. "Great. Tell her hi for me. The praise band is doing some stuff at the eleven o'clock service. I guess if you're going to that one I better let you go." We talked a short while longer and I even got expressions of love out of my son. Once I hung up I realized we hadn't talked about his ratty goatee. But then if Hal had given somebody a ring on Christmas Eve, Grandma Lillian probably had enough to deal with that she might not be paying that much attention to Ben's face.

The Morgans' house was dimly lit when I drove past on my way to church. I knew that the family, including Candace, had gone to an earlier service. Dot had stopped by afterward to tell me that she'd heard through the grapevine that Matt was out of critical care and alert enough to talk to the police, which probably meant Ray. Matt wasn't out of the woods yet, but the doctors thought that he probably wouldn't have a lot of lasting damage from the skull fracture Tracy Collins had inflicted on him. It was the best news we could expect at this point.

Stars twinkled in the clear sky above Rancho Conejo and the air had just enough bite to make it feel almost like Christmas at home. The difference was that by ten o'clock tomorrow morning I wouldn't need a coat and an ice scraper for my windshield. Knowing that, it was good to walk through the church parking lot, watching my breath make a cloud when I exhaled.

Inside the church the smell of evergreen filled the sanctuary. Lots of people had gotten here ahead of me. I made my way to the front first for a quick hello to Cai Li. She gave me an enthusiastic hug before I headed back to look for a seat in the empty spots of the back rows. Off to one side I saw people I definitely wanted to sit next to. Estella and Lucy Perez sat with an infant seat between them, and I came and got the empty chair next to Lucy. "I'm so glad that you're here," I told her, watching her smile shyly.

"Me, too. I wanted to come back for Christmas. This is the right place to be."

Estella gave a wry smile. "We're up every couple of hours anyway, so we figured the late service fit in real well. I hope it's okay that we came here."

"Of course. Everybody's welcome here. Lucy could tell you that." I looked over into the infant carrier where the baby snoozed peacefully in a tiny bright pink stretchy suit. She had plenty of dark hair like her mother and aunt, and a few days' time had given her a chance to look much less red and scrunched up. "What have you named her?"

"Carmen for her grandmother, but we've been calling her something else," Estella said.

Lucy reached out one finger and stroked her daughter's velvet cheek. *"Milagrita,"* she said softly.

I know just enough Spanish by now to know that Carmen's other name meant "little miracle." It felt so appropriate in this season of miracles and birth we'd all been waiting for.

The last month had started with death and horror for all of us. We'd come so far in four weeks, and now the month was ending in miracles large and small in the warmth of candle glow and music. Even though all my sisters in Christ weren't here with me I felt surrounded by their love. It was the feeling that kept me coming back here.

"That's wonderful," I told Lucy. Little miracle. It summed up perfectly that grace-full place we all came to on this Christmas Eve. As the service started I watched the sleeping infant, knowing she'd already lived up to her name.

Center Point Publishing
600 Brooks Road ● PO Box 1
Thorndike ME 04986-0001 USA

(207) 568-3717

US & Canada:
1 800 929-9108